Clues Over Croissants

A Bess Bullock Retirement Home Mystery

by

Allen B. Boyer

For information, email **Cozy Cat Press**, cozycatpress@aol.com or visit our website at: www.cozycatpress.com

COZY CAT
PRESS

ISBN: 978-0-9848402-5-0
Printed in the United States of America

Cover design by Cecilia Rockwell
http://coversbycecilia.daportfolio.com   ,

10 9 8 7 6 5 4 3 2 1

For my dear wife, the sweetest rose in the garden of my heart.

LIES AND STAINS

Bess Bullock always began her day with the same kind of breakfast: a bowl of oatmeal, half a banana, juice and a well-buttered English muffin. It was a breakfast routine as consistent and reliable as the days she experienced since moving into the Honey Hills Retirement Center. After all, she told herself, consistency and reliance were two of the things she was paying for. Bess had weathered a life of unpredictability as a wife, a mother, and the only female police officer in the neighboring town of Venton. Now well into her retirement years, and having just turned eighty, Bess was ready for a more simple life of predictability and routine. Such days usually began with the same breakfast. This morning, as Bess sat down at her table in the dining hall, she quickly noticed two things disrupting the consistency of her day.

To her left, Bess found a new face sitting at her table. A fresh face joined Abbey Toomey and Clara Carson, the other two ladies who shared three meals a day with Bess. While the dining hall had a casual atmosphere, Bess found the assigned seating a bit constraining. After a few meals, there was little to learn about the two ladies assigned to sit with Bess. However, this morning presented something different. There was a new face to get to know. Bess let her eyes move across the woman's kindly smile, narrow glasses and short white hair. Bess continued to study the new person's small face, her narrow neck, and the gold bracelets that loosely dangled from both of her slender wrists. Bess finally decided to offer some sort of greeting to her new table mate.

"Good morning," Bess smiled. "My name is Bess Bullock."

"Minnie Darcy," the woman replied, without so much as a smile.

The lack of reaction caused Bess to turn her eyes down to the table. She let her eyes glide around the place settings before stopping at her own. In less than a minute, Bess had noticed something else that was different at the breakfast table. While her bowl of oatmeal, juice, and banana were all present, there was also an empty saucer dish with crumbs on it. An empty dish where, Bess presumed, her muffin had been resting.

"My muffin," Bess said, looking around the table. "Did everyone get a muffin? I seem to be missing mine."

"I have mine," Abbey Toomey dutifully reported.

"I have one too, Bess," Clara Carson said. She picked the muffin up from the dish and held it in the air like a small prize. "Would you like mine?"

"No, thank you," Bess replied, raising her hand to Clara. "It's just unusual. I always have a muffin for breakfast. To my recollection, I don't think I've ever come in here and not found my juice, oatmeal, banana, and muffin waiting for me. It's a mystery to me as to why it's not here."

Automatically the word "mystery" triggered a switch in Bess. It fired up the instincts that had served her so well as the first female police officer in her hometown of Venton. Yes, Bess smiled, this was a little thing. Life was full of little mysteries. Where was the fun in not solving one?

Her eyes began to study the table more carefully. She noticed the bright white napkins at each place setting. She could see how every napkin had been folded and fixed beside a dish. Then she noted how each napkin was folded into the shape of a triangle, except for one. Bess found her eyes lingering on that one napkin, which was set in front of the new person, Minnie Darcy. Minnie was the only person at the table who had nothing to say in reply to Bess's inquiry into the whereabouts of her muffin. Minnie was sitting right next to Bess, quietly staring straight ahead. Bess lowered her gaze and looked at Minnie's napkin again.

"Minnie," Bess began, and she pointed her finger at Minnie's napkin. "I cannot help but notice that your napkin has a stain in the middle of it. A small round yellow stain. I can tell you put it there because your napkin is not folded into a triangle like the others. Your napkin looks more like a square...as if you used it briefly to wipe up something and then hastily placed it next to your plate again. I also see a similar drop on the white table cloth between your place setting and mine. I suspect that the two stains, if I smelled them, were butter stains that came when you dropped my muffin."

Bess then placed her hand on the table cloth and gently ran it across the surface. When she lifted her hand up, she found a few crumbs sticking to the palm of her hand. She sat up in her seat, turned to Minnie, and showed her the crumbs.

"Did you eat my muffin, Minnie?" Bess asked.

"Of course, not," Minnie quickly answered without looking at Bess.

"Let me tell you something, my dear," Bess said, raising her gaze from Minnie's napkin to her face. "These table clothes are spotless for breakfast...and yet I was still able to find bread crumbs that I suspect belonged to my wayward muffin between your plate and mine. You have butter on your napkin and on the table cloth between our place settings. Anyone who eats in here knows the muffins they provide for breakfast are already buttered when served. The butter is melted and rather warm. A new person might not have known that, thus causing the butter to spill out the sides when eaten."

Bess paused for a moment to give Minnie the opportunity to say something. Minnie simply looked around the room, refusing to acknowledge Bess or her words.

"Now you've been assigned to sit with us," Bess pointed out. "You may be here for a few months. I know these ladies because we've shared meals for well over a year. I know they are honest with me as I am with them. You, on the other hand, have a butter stain on your napkin, a butter stain on the table cloth next to your plate, and the more I look at your face the more I realize you also have bread crumbs on the corners of your mouth that match the crumbs on the table. Since you still have your muffin, this leads me to conclude that you ate a muffin before any of us arrived. Since I am the only party here without a muffin, my conclusion is that you ate mine for some strange reason and are now trying to lie about it."

Bess sat back in her seat and took a deep breath. It felt good to put all of her little observations together into one clear conclusion.

"She used to be a police officer," Clara Carson said from across the table to Minnie.

"You better give her *your* muffin…if you know what's good for you."

"Here," Minnie said, handing the muffin over to Bess. "Take it. I don't care."

Bess calmly stared at the muffin and waved her hand at Minnie to keep it. She took a sip of her juice and now stared at Minnie with a clear unblinking gaze.

"I don't care about the muffin," Bess explained. "What I care about is honesty. We share this table three times a day for meals. I have enjoyed talking to Clara and Abbey and they have enjoyed sharing stories with me. Honesty is at the center of what we share at this table. You've been assigned to this table to share meals with us, Minnie. If you cannot be honest with us, we will not include you in our conversations. Do you understand?"

Minnie quietly nodded in reply. Her eyes were still down and then she looked at Bess and the other ladies at the table. She closed her eyes, let out a sigh, and tilted her head to one side.

"I was just so hungry...I'm sorry I ate your muffin," she sighed.

"Apology accepted," Bess smiled and she took another sip of her juice. She leaned in, took a bite of her cereal, and said, "Now...let's enjoy breakfast and get to know each other a little better."

THE LAST ATTACHMENT

Later in the morning Bess sat in her room reflecting on Minnie and how quickly she was able to draw her conclusions about the missing muffin. While she thought back on breakfast, she was reminded of how the smallest detail could not escape her investigative instincts. She had been the first female police officer in her hometown of Venton. Her instincts would never let her forget it. She found herself smiling when she recalled the look on Minnie's face when she heard a soft knock on her door.

"Come in," Bess called out, shifting her eyes to the door.

Her daughter, Samantha, entered the room with her cell phone in the familiar position of being nestled to her ear. She raised one finger in the air to Bess and spoke quickly into the small cell phone that seemed to always be clutched in her hand. Bess could make out the word "house" and the word "mother" and quickly deduced what the phone call was about. She watched her daughter smile and offer a few words to wrap up the conversation. Then, quite suddenly, Samantha pulled the phone away from her ear, snapped it shut and stepped into the room.

"I have good news, mother. That was the realtor on the phone. We have someone who will buy the house," Samantha reported. She pushed her long dark hair back over her shoulders and smiled. "They've agreed to pay what you want...not a penny less. If you could come with me, Mom, we could sign some papers at the realtor's office and wrap this up by noon."

Bess forced herself to smile at Samantha's news. It seemed to her that her daughter was always focused on "wrapping up" matters and not pausing to appreciate the significance of what was happening. This was one of those times. Bess had held onto her house when she moved to the Honey Hills Retirement Center just over a year ago. It was an emotional attachment that helped her to think of her move as some kind of vacation. Honey Hills was a temporary respite, Bess told herself. It was a temporary respite before returning home. When her daughter spoke to her about selling the house, Bess agreed but set the price so high she doubted anyone would pay full price. After being on the market for more than a year, someone had finally agreed to the price Bess set. While Samantha looked quite happy about the development, Bess was not in the mood to celebrate. Samantha helped Bess out of her chair.

"After you sign the papers," Samantha grinned, grabbing a sweater for Bess, "I'm going to take you out for a celebration lunch. When the realtor called...Mom, I almost jumped up and down. I mean...the house has been for sale for so long. I just never thought anyone would want it. Do you know how lucky we are?"

"It's a good home," Bess mumbled.

"The realtor said it's a young couple," Samantha said, helping Bess out of her chair.

"They have children...so there will be a young family living in the house. I thought that would make you happy."

"Take me to my house," Bess said, slipping on her sweater. "Before we sign the papers...take me to my house."

"I'm not sure if we have time," Samantha said, glancing at her watch.

"I want to see my house one more time," Bess pressed, and she ended the statement with a steely gaze that she used to give Samantha when she was two feet shorter and many years younger.

"Take me to my house, Samantha."

Soon Bess found herself standing in front of a narrow red brick building in a suburban neighborhood of Venton. The grass, which Bess employed someone to cut, was crisp and green and speckled with bright yellow dandelions. Bess followed the narrow walkway that wound under a large oak tree before stopping at the front porch. She laid her hand on the black iron railing that accompanied a short flight of steps to the porch. She slipped her key into the lock, turned it and stepped inside.

"We only have a few minutes," Samantha announced from the porch, nervously checking her watch again.

"Wait here," Bess instructed, before closing the door.

She stepped into the main room, her shoes clapping on the hardwood floor. She sniffed the stale air, looked at all her old furniture and smiled.

"Every room has a story," Bess told herself.

She soon found herself standing in the living room where she and her husband would set up their Christmas tree in the winter, watch the New Year change on the television, and play on the floor with baby Samantha. In one corner, Bess could still see Samantha taking her first steps.

Bess walked down a hallway and lingered by the door to one small bedroom. As she stood in the doorway, Bess could still hear Samantha as a child speaking about the nightmares that woke her in her bedroom. There were many nights when Bess came into this room to calm her daughter down from the "bad bug dreams" that always woke her.

Bess turned and walked down to another room. This time she stopped and looked at a large bed and matching dresser in a master bedroom. A memory jumped forth and Bess could see her husband reading in the bed, as he always did before going to sleep. She could also see them in bed together, reviewing the events of the day and sharing their hopes for the future while they stared into the darkness.

Bess moved downstairs to the kitchen where she had spent many hours cooking and baking and filling the air with wonderful fragrances that settled in every room. She ran her hand over the basement door and thought about all the projects her husband worked on down there. All the things in the house that he fixed and all the things he meant to fix. She thought about the many tools that were probably still on his work bench waiting for him. He was not the best at doing things around the house, Bess recalled, but he was not the worst either.

Finally, she walked over to a window where she remembered standing and looking out during the dark days when her baby son died. His name was Adam and he lived for only a few hours, but Bess spent years staring out that window thinking about all the missed possibilities of his future and what had been lost.

The floors creaked when she walked on them. The walls still held photos of a younger Bullock family that had once led full happy days in this house. Bess paused in front of one of the photos and touched the cool glass with her fingers. She gazed into the eyes of her much younger face smiling back.

Her steps were small and measured and her eyes danced around every room, lingering on different spots.

There was a story in every room, and her memories were vividly ignited by this final trip to her house.

After a few minutes, she paused at the front door. She drew in her breath, and she could not help but smile. It was like the air was filled with little feathers that tickled her. She would leave the walls, the windows, the ceiling and the floors for the next owners. She would take the memories, the stories, and the past with her. They were the only things left to care about in this house.

THE LEFT FOOTED PROBLEM

One of the activities that Bess enjoyed most at the Honey Hills Retirement Center was participating in a dance club.   The Honey Hills Center Waltzing Club was made up of a group of residents that consisted of men and women who enjoyed gliding around on a dance floor one morning a week.   While a good many of the members who belonged to the club were married, a few of the members were widowed like Bess.

"Okay everyone," Chet Wooden, the president of the Waltzing Club, announced.   Chet was a tall lean man with white hair that was always combed to the side, and glasses that magnified his bright blue eyes. He was also a widower.   Bess watched him step to the middle of the room and in his soft voice began the meeting.   "We have a new step to learn this morning.   I need some music and my favorite dance partner.   Come here, Bess."

Chet quickly snatched Bess by the hand, as he usually did at their meetings, and together they went out on the dance floor to demonstrate a new dance.   Music filled the room.   Chet led, as he always did, and Bess kept up with his steps and his moves.   It was a challenge to anticipate his actions on a dance floor, but Bess was always up to the task.   Soon other couples, some married and some not, were swirling around them on the dance floor.   They all moved with smiles as broad as the one Bess wore when she danced with Chet.

Because so many of the members were couples, Bess often found herself paired up with Chet.   After a year of dancing together, Bess soon realized that her chemistry with Chet was spilling into their personal lives, too. This mutual flirtation culminated when Chet joined Bess for a plane ride to celebrate her eightieth birthday. It was in this small airplane, while flying over a mountain bursting with bright fall foliage, that Chet leaned over and kissed Bess for the first time. The kiss was a launching point for months of long walks, hand holding and enjoying each other's company. Dancing, talking, and laughing with Chet gave Bess a sense of fulfillment in her days at Honey Hills. A widow for many years, her heart welcomed the feelings that came from such actions. However, things between Chet and Bess started to change. Bess could easily remember the day it happened. It was the day that a woman named Lillian Peck arrived for a meeting of the Waltzing Club.

At first, Lillian appeared to be a pleasant woman with a ready smile and a cheerful personality. Bess found Lillian to be quite charming when she first began to come to the meetings. Bess also noticed that Lillian had two left feet on the dance floor. Quite often Lillian would stumble or completely surrender to any fancy footwork that came with a new dance step. Whenever she got far behind the rest of the group, Lillian would always stop dancing, stand perfectly still on the dance floor and ask the same person to help her.

"Chet!" Lillian's voice called out as it usually did during a meeting. "I'm afraid this step is too difficult. Can you help me, Chet?"

Bess turned to see Lillian walking off the dance floor shaking her head. Chet let go of Bess, as he usually did whenever Lillian called his name or grew defeated over a new dance.

"I'm sorry, Bess," Chet apologized.

"It's okay," Bess nodded and smiled when he stepped away. "You're the president. It's your job to help the other members of the club."

In the beginning, Bess told herself that because Chet was the president of the waltzing club it was his duty to help Lillian with all the fancy steps they were learning. For all her calls for help, it was always Chet who would come to Lillian's rescue and show her the right way to step or move until she got it right. Then one morning, Bess watched Chet help Lillian with a move that required them to dance cheek to cheek. She watched his hands move around her waist and then together they high stepped around the floor in perfect unison.

"They move so nicely together," Bess heard one woman say to another.

Bess felt her face grow hot after hearing those words. She found her eyes fluttering around Chet as she watched him smile at Lillian. Bess knew he was smiling to put Lillian at ease, but then she watched Chet's hand slide around Lillian's waist. Bess noticed how he spoke to her and how Lillian spoke back and how they both laughed at the same time. Bess could feel her face grow hot while she watched them. Her heart was pounding. She could tell her face was turning red. She could feel her anger growing towards a woman she barely knew. All of these things led Bess to a conclusion that she could hardly believe.

For the first time since she was a young girl in love, Bess was feeling a sense of jealousy towards Lillian. At first, Bess could barely recognize the emotion. When she finally realized she was jealous, Bess felt ashamed by what emotion her heart was brewing. The fact she could still feel jealous about something at her age led Bess to reflect on the emotion for the rest of the day.

She was almost embarrassed to admit it, but she loved Chet and she didn't want to lose him. She hoped her feelings about Lillian were wrong. She hoped she truly was just a bad dancer and nothing more. Bess longed to know the real intentions of this newest member to the Waltzing Club. How would she find out the truth?

CARDS AND QUESTIONS

When she first moved to Honey Hills, Bess Bullock was invited to participate in a rather unusual club. It was a Bridge Club comprised of Bess and three other ladies. Every Tuesday morning, the four women would gather to play cards and chat about their daily adventures at the Honey Hills Retirement Center. This morning Bess found herself walking with a sense of purpose to the meeting. She wasn't walking quickly because she was excited about playing cards. She was interested in learning more about Lillian Peck. She had some questions she wanted to ask and was curious to discover what kinds of insights her friends would share.

Bess followed the hallway around the corners and then stopped at a brightly lit room filled with tables and a shelving unit on the wall. The shelves contained card games, board games and even some boxes of puzzles. When she opened the door, Bess found that the Bridge Club was in full attendance. Rose Grumbine, Flo Morgenstern and Alma Crisp were already seated around a narrow table, waiting for Bess to join them. Bess sat down and looked across the table at Flo who began to shuffle cards for the first game of the morning.

"Morning, Bess," Alma smiled.

"Morning everyone," Bess said in a soft tone of voice.

"Now that we're all here," Flo said, holding up a deck of cards in one hand. "I'm ready to deal...are we ready to play, ladies?"

"I think so," Rose replied with a knowing glance around the table.

Without hesitation, Flo began to deal the cards and the first round of bridge had begun. Bess watched each dealt card slide across the well polished table top and slow down just in front of the person who was intended to receive it. Bess always marveled at Flo's control over dealing cards. Years of work as a Black Jack dealer for a casino in Atlantic City provided Flo with the necessary skills to get the cards to obey her will.

For the first few minutes, no one spoke and the cards moved quickly around the table. Each woman picked up her cards and began to examine them. No one spoke as they indulged in the pleasure of playing the game. Bess couldn't help but notice that the silence in the room, or the intensity of the first game, was dampening the flow of conversation between herself and her friends. Finally, after a few minutes of silent card playing, Bess decided to open the table to a topic of conversation she was quite anxious to share.

"Do any of you know Lillian Peck?" Bess asked.

"She's new," Rose quickly answered, keeping her cards in front of her face. "She started coming to one of our book clubs about a month ago. I believe she said she's from New York."

"Don't know her," Flo mumbled. "Unless she plays cards or Bingo...I don't know her."

"I'm afraid I don't know her either," Alma said with an almost apologetic tone.

"There's something about her," Bess sighed and she lowered her cards. "I can't quite put my finger on it. She comes to the Waltzing Club meetings. When she first started to come she told everyone how much she loves to dance...but she is quite helpless on the dance floor. She can't do any dance moves without help. In fact, she's always apologizing because she needs Chet to assist her all the time. Most of us who are members are good dancers and we formed the club because we enjoy the experience. It wasn't intended to become a dance school. Why do you think she keeps coming to Waltzing Club if she can't dance? I just think it's very strange."

"Well, Bess," Rose said, sorting out the cards in her hand. "I think you may have answered your own question."

"How?" Bess asked, feeling a sense of confusion that caused her to lower her cards.

"You said she always needs Chet around..." Rose smiled.

"You said she needs him...all the time," Alma joined in with another small grin.

"Oh for heaven's sake, Bess, do we have to spell it out?" Flo grumbled while she organized the cards in her hand. "She likes Chet. You said she wants him to help her all the time. That's why she's coming to your Waltzing Club...not because of the dancing...because she wants Chet's attention."

"You think so?" Bess asked, sitting up a little straighter in her seat.

Suddenly all the pieces were coming together. The way Lillian would call Chet over. The way Lillian would smile and laugh so frequently when Chet assisted her with a dance or a move. The way she'd keep her eyes on him whenever he danced with Bess. It was in this moment of enlightenment that Bess could feel a great swell of jealousy come over her. Bess now realized it wasn't her instincts speaking badly about Lillian. It was her heart.

"How would I know for sure?" Bess asked, tapping her cards on the table.

"Talk to her," Rose suggested. "She's a woman. You're a woman. Confront her about her feelings for Chet and see what she says."

"I suppose I could…it's just…I…" Bess mumbled.

"Good heavens, Bess," Flo snapped. "Aren't you the big detective in this place? The person who solves mysteries for everyone around here? Tell me you couldn't figure this one out without us helping you?"

"I'm afraid I wouldn't have," Bess confessed. She leaned forward a little like she was about to reveal a secret. "You see, ladies…I've noticed that the mysteries in my life are the hardest ones to solve. Other people's problems are easier for me to examine. I don't know why…but that's just how life is for me."

"When I have problems, I find that sharing them with my friends is the best method I have for solving them," Alma stated.

"Me too," Rose nodded. "It's one reason why we have our group, ladies. We all have problems from time to time and it's good to have each other to share them. Yes, Bess, you are good at solving mysteries…but I'm glad you let us share in your problems, too."

"Thank you," Bess smiled.

"Good luck with Lillian," Rose said.

"Yes. Now can we please get back to playing cards, ladies?" Flo asked before raising her cards and tossing one of them onto the table.

As the cards and the bridge games flew by, Bess couldn't help but think about the right words she would use to confront Lillian Peck.

A CHANGE IN OLIVE CRUMBLY

The days drifted by and Bess still had not spoken to Lillian. Most days at the Honey Hills Center went by with very little variation. Bess often found that one day was a carbon copy of another day. Meals were served as scheduled. Pills were consumed at the same time. The usual nurses roamed the hallways at the same hour of every day. It was a quality about the Honey Hills Center that Bess didn't like, but she knew it was what she and the other residents were paying for. One resident in particular seemed to thrive on such consistency. Her name was Olive Crumbly.

Day after day, Olive roamed the hallways with very little expression on her face. Her lips were always set and closed. Her eyes never narrowed or widened. When she spoke, it was with little variation in volume or tone. Indeed, Bess once thought, Olive was as reliable as the days at the Honey Hills Center…days that were so similar, so monotonous, so exact that they seemed to blur together.

Yet, to see Olive and her unwavering appearance was only half the experience. One had to merely speak to Olive to truly understand why her face was rarely graced with a smile. Whatever the topic of conversation, Olive would always turn the dialogue towards her dead husband.

Bess could recall one occasion when they were watching a baseball game on TV. When Bess commented on the color of the player's uniforms, Olive replied, "My husband used to watch sports...of course he died a few years ago."

On another occasion, Bess found Olive seated in a chair just outside of the dining room reading a newspaper. Bess pointed to the front page article about the local elections and made an observation about one of the candidates. Over the next few minutes, a conversation blossomed on everything from the candidates, to the issues, to the weather for election day. Just as Bess was about to leave, Olive quickly added, "My husband used to help tabulate the elections where we lived....of course he died a few years ago."

Even a passing comment by Bess about the nice weather outside brought about yet another response from Olive about her dearly departed husband.

"My husband used to do the gardening in our yard on days like this," Olive sighed. "Of course, he died a few years ago."

There was no doubt about it, Bess thought, Olive Crumbly was half a person without her husband. Of course, there were other women at the Honey Hills Center who were widows, too. Other women who, like Bess, had lost good men. Yet, most of the women Bess knew managed to continue on with their lives. They found hobbies, or activities, or friends to help fill their days and their hearts. Bess felt quite fortunate to be one of these women. Yet, there were also women like Olive. Women who were unable, or disinterested, in replacing the void left by a deceased spouse. Women who carried a grief that they preferred to wear and share with others. Olive Crumbly was one such person.

Lately, Bess had noticed something different about Olive when she saw her in the hallways, the dining room, or even the game room. Olive's lips were turned up and not down in her usual scowl. Her cheeks were no longer flat on her face but pushed up under her sparkling eyes. She was wearing what appeared to be a smile, which made Olive quite unrecognizable to Bess. She noted the change more than once, and like any good investigator, Bess became curious about the change in Olive's demeanor.

One day she spotted Olive seated on a couch next to a window in the hallway. Bess sat down beside Olive, smiled, and joined her in staring out the window. The sun was bright and it appeared to be another hot summer day. In the distance, green stalks of corn filled a nearby farmer's field.

"Looks like the corn is getting taller," Bess observed.

"It looks pretty," Olive smiled. "I love coming here in the mornings and looking at it."

"I also enjoy looking at the farms around here," Bess replied. "I especially enjoy watching the horses in the field. They're so graceful and yet so strong when they work. There's a window down by the Dementia Wing with a beautiful view of the horses."

"I know that window," Olive said, standing up. "Some day I'd like to go out and stand at the fence. I'd love to just watch the horses up close. I bet they're beautiful to watch in person.

Well, I've got to go, Bess. Nice talking to you."

As she watched Olive walk away, Bess suddenly realized something quite surprising.

For the first time in the nearly two years of talking to Olive Crumbly, Bess had just completed a conversation with her in which she didn't mention her dead husband. That, plus her unwavering smile, now caused Bess's instincts to rise up and speak to her in a loud, crisp voice. There was indeed something different about Olive. Bess wanted to find out what had caused her to change.

"Olive Crumbly seems rather happy these days," Bess announced at her Tuesday morning Bridge Club meeting. The comment was met with silence from Flo, Alma and Rose, who all seemed more focused on their cards than the words Bess spoke.

"Has anyone else noticed how happy Olive seems to be?" Bess asked again.

"So she's happy," Flo mumbled. "Maybe they switched her medication. I've seen that happen to some people. I think it's nice to see Olive smile in the hallway for a change. She looks better without that glum expression on her face."

"Yes," Rose chimed in, "I agree with Flo. It is nice to see Olive smiling. If anyone deserves to be a little happy it's Olive."

"It is nice to see her happy, but..." Bess began, but then found her words were interrupted. She could feel her investigative instincts ignite and her mind began to race with possible explanations.

"Bess," Alma began. "There's nothing wrong with being happy. Why would you consider someone's happiness a matter for investigation?"

"It's what I've seen," Bess stated. She sat back and put her cards down on the table. She thought back on her observations of Olive and then looked around at her friends. "For example, most people will smile at something around them, like a friendly face, a pleasant smell, or even a box of chocolates. Olive seems to be smiling at...nothing. I have observed her sitting by herself with no one else around and she simply smiles to herself and mumbles on occasion. I have seen her walking around the hallways, smiling at no one in particular. I've seen her enter and leave the dining hall with a smile on her face. That includes the occasions when we are served meat loaf. How anyone can bare to smile with that horrid aroma of meat loaf in the air is beyond me."

"I agree," Alma chimed in. "The meatloaf really is quite bad. We all know Chef Frank doesn't make a good meatloaf."

"Or anything else for that matter," Flo mumbled.

"I think you're making much out of nothing," Alma said with a wave of her hand. "Olive is happy…leave it at that."

"Perhaps," Bess replied. "I plan to follow my instincts, ladies, and see where they lead me. First, I will need to confront Olive."

"So you're going to walk up and say, "Excuse me, Olive, I was wondering why you're so happy?" Is that how you plan to confront her?" Flo laughed

Bess glared at Flo and she could feel eyebrows fold together. Flo's condescending tone and words were making Bess's blood boil, but Bess took a deep breath and remained calm.

"Flo," Rose Grumbine finally spoke for the first time on the matter. "We know that Bess has investigated many matters here at the Honey Hills Center. Most of her investigations have led to satisfactory resolutions. I think if she suspects something is wrong with Olive, she should look into it."

"I plan on doing just that," Bess said, and she stood up and stepped away from the table.

Later in the afternoon, Bess found herself standing in front of Olive Crumbly's door. Flo's words still hung in her mind. Indeed, how would she explain her presence to Olive? What reason would she give for coming to visit a person she rarely spoke to in social scenes? Bess closed her fist, drew in a deep breath and hoped that instinct would guide her once she was inside. She knocked on the door twice, then lowered her head and waited for a response. She watched the door knob turn and looked up to see Olive's face appear.

"Good morning, Bess," Olive smiled. "Nice to see you."

"I was walking by and I thought I'd just stop to say hello," Bess responded.

"That was very nice," Olive said, stepping into the hallway.

Bess glanced over Olive's shoulder inside her room. Her bed was neatly made. Her television was on and a leather chair sat in front of it. Bess could tell by the creases in the leather that Olive had been sitting there before she answered the door. Bess let her eyes drift to the floor where something caught her attention. It was something small and out of place from the rest of the décor of the room.

"I believe you dropped something on the floor," Bess said, pointing over Olive's shoulder.

"That?" Olive said, turning and looking back at Bess. Her smile was no longer on her face and she grabbed Bess's hand and quickly pulled her into the room. "Can you keep a secret, Bess?"

"Of course," Bess answered, her eyes quickly scanning the room she now found herself standing in. A sweater was draped over the back of a chair. A quilt was neatly folded on a bed. Assorted jewelry was piled in a small wooden jewelry box on a dresser. Everything appeared to look normal and in its proper place. Then her eyes were drawn back to the one item that appeared out of place; the small silver bowl that sat on the floor under the window.

"I have a little friend," Olive whispered. She topped off her confession with the broadest smile Bess had ever seen her make. "He comes to visit me at night. He comes right through that window to visit me."

Bess turned her eyes to the window that Olive pointed to. There was a small hole in the screen that covered the window. A hole that was too small for a man to climb through.

"What sort of visitor are you talking about?" Bess asked, stepping closer to the window.

"A cat," Olive softly replied. "I call him Francis. I had a cat just like Francis when I was a girl. He's golden from head to tail with a drip of white fur on his chest. He's just a beautiful cat., Bess I don't know where he comes from, but I'm quite certain he likes me."

"I see." Bess nodded. So this would explain the change in behavior, the more frequent smiles, and the good mood that seemed to have settled over Olive. Indeed, it was her love for a cat that had finally filled the void left by her husband. After many years, Bess thought, Olive had something to love again.

"I knew I could tell you," Olive said. "The other residents talk about how you investigate things and how you can keep a secret. Will you be able to keep my secret?"

"Of course," Bess answered with a smile. "He probably belongs on one of the nearby farms. Just remember that pets aren't allowed in the Honey Hills Center, Olive. The nurses might not be too happy if they walked in and found Francis in your bed."

"He actually prefers to stay under my bed," Olive pointed out. "I keep a towel under there for him to sleep on. The nurses wouldn't notice it."

Bess nodded at the comment. Her eyes went to the bed and she could see a corner of a pink towel sticking out from under the bed.

"Very well," Bess answered. "I've got to get going, Olive. I'll see you at the dining hall for supper."

"I believe it will be meat loaf for dinner tonight," Olive grinned. "Oh how I do love meat loaf."

Bess stepped out of the room happy to have discovered a resolution to her concerns, but unhappy to learn that Chef Frank had put meat loaf on the menu again.

As she prepared for bed that night, the taste of meatloaf was fresh in Bess's mouth. She brushed her teeth twice and still couldn't get rid of the flavor. She thought about brushing them a third time, but then tried to think of something else. Olive Crumbly's face flashed in her mind. Bess thought about whether Olive's feline visitor was actually in her room right now. In her mind, she could see Olive sleeping with a smile on her face, knowing that her furry friend was curled up on a blanket under her bed. Love often caused people to smile randomly throughout the day. Her feelings for Chet actually caused Bess to smile in the hallways, or on her morning walks, or just sitting in her room by herself. Of course, she thought, Olive's love for this cat had filled a void in her heart. A void left by her husband. Now that she knew why Olive was happy, Bess felt a certain sense of peace as she drifted off to sleep.

A loud noise woke Bess in the middle of the night. It was not the most pleasant way to wake up, but a loud noise is never the most preferential way to return from a deep sleep. Bess shook her head, looked around, grabbed her glasses and heard the noise again. It sounded like someone was hammering a nail into her door. Bess managed to turn on the light next to her bed and swing her legs out from under the covers.

"Two in the morning," she yawned after looking at her clock. "Who could be up this late at night?"

She tucked her feet into her slippers, stood up, and gave herself a few seconds to gather her balance. Her knees cracked, as they always did when she took her first steps after getting out of bed. She slipped on her robe as another loud knock filled the room. Bess shuffled across the floor and right for the door. When she opened the door, she found Olive Crumbly standing in the doorway. Bess noticed that Olive's face had returned to its normal contortions; a broad scowl stretched under two blue eyes that appeared to be red and teary.

"Olive," Bess managed to say, "It's quite late. What's the matter?"

"It's Francis," Olive managed to say and her eyes began to blink quite fast. "He's slipped out of my room, Bess. I don't know where he went. I'm afraid he's loose somewhere in the Honey Hills Center. Can you help me find him?"

Bess yawned and looked back in her room at the clock that was reminding her of the late hour. She yawned and turned back to look at her late night guest standing in the doorway.

"Olive," Bess began. "I'm really quite tired."

"Please," Olive begged. "You're the only person I told about Francis. You're the only one I can ask for help."

The expression on Olive's face was one of sheer panic. She was genuinely scared about losing Francis. If she were in a similar situation, Bess thought, she would want someone to help her too. The nurses could be quite nasty about breaking rules, especially the ones involving a pet. Bess drew in her breath, looked back at her warm bed, then slipped on a robe and tied it shut. She turned to Olive and managed to muster a smile.

"Shall we go back to your room and start from there?" Bess suggested.

"Thank you," Olive replied, her scowl turning up into a smile.

Bess and Olive quietly moved down the dimly lit hallways, avoiding the places where Bess knew there were nurses' stationed. Soon Bess was back at Olive's room. They stood in the doorway and Bess looked at Olive. Olive's eyes were wide and darting around the floor and her bottom lip was now tucked under her teeth. Bess smiled and rubbed Olive's arm with her hand.

"So which way did Francis go from here?" Bess asked.

"That way," Olive stated, pointing down one of the hallways. She drew her hands together in front of her waist and squeezed them tightly. "Oh I hope Francis is okay. He was so quick I just couldn't close my door fast enough."

"It'll be okay," Bess said, and she gave Olive's hand a gentle squeeze. She waved her hand down the hallway. "Most of the doors are closed at this time of night. With these long halls, we should be able to find Francis."

As they walked, Bess couldn't help but think how time seemed to come to a standstill at night. There were no people to pass in the hallways of Honey Hills. No one to talk to. No activities of any kind to hear or see. There was only darkness, silence, and complete stillness. Bess entertained these thoughts while she and Olive walked up and down the hallways scanning the floors for any sign of a cat.

As they studied each hall, Bess offered a few words of comfort to Olive. Yet, no matter what she said, Olive remained silent and her eyes darted from side to side. While Olive kept her eyes down, Bess would look up from time to time for a stray nurse to appear. She knew any nurse would question why two residents were roaming the hallways so late at night. Bess kept thinking of what to say to such an inquiry. There were fewer nurses on duty during the overnight hours as compared to the day. The ones that tended to work overnight were young and new to the Honey Hills Center. Bess felt that the odds of running into one of them were remote. Just as she was feeling good about their odds, Bess looked down one hallway to find a nurse walking in their direction. The nurse made eye contact and picked up her pace.

"Ladies!" she called out. "Why are you up so late? What do you need?"

Bess drew in her breath and looked at Olive.

"What should we do?" Olive asked.

"Keep going," Bess said, pushing Olive down a side hall. "I'll take care of the nurse. Go check in the dining room. If he's hungry, Francis might have smelled something to eat in the kitchen. He might have even found some scraps of food on the floor. Check there and I'll catch up to you."

"Good idea," Olive said, turning and walking away with a spring in her step.

While she watched Olive move down the hall, Bess began to think about what to say to the nurse at hand. How could she phrase this in a way that wouldn't get Olive in trouble? She watched the young nurse quickly approach, her blond ponytail bobbing with each step.

"Why are you ladies up?" the nurse asked. "Are you lost? Do you need help getting back to your room? Where's your friend?"

Bess guessed this nurse was in her twenties, but noticed how she spoke with the kind of sharp tone of someone much older. Bess watched the young nurse check her watch and then look down the hallway for Olive.

"Do you know what time it is?" the nurse asked. "You both should be in bed."

"You're right," Bess smiled. "We both know it's late. You see, my friend said that she thought she spotted a cat running loose in the hallways. I believe the cat woke her up. She came to my room asking for help in finding the cat. I was merely trying to help her catch it."

It was a viable story, Bess thought. The cat was loose and if they found it, Bess and Olive could use it as evidence to support their story. Bess guessed Olive was smart enough not to lay claim to the cat with a nurse present. If the cat got away, Olive was no longer in trouble for breaking the rules.

"A cat?" the nurse asked and her head tilted to the side, flinging her blond ponytail over one shoulder. "I haven't seen any cat around here."

"I'm simply telling you what she told me," Bess said. "She came to my room and asked for my help in finding a stray cat. Being a good friend I agreed to help."

"Where is your friend?" the nurse asked.

"She was going to check in the dining room for that cat," Bess said.

Together Bess and the nurse walked at a brisk pace. The young nurse took the lead, while Bess trailed behind. She hoped she had chosen the right words to keep Olive from getting into trouble. When they reached the dining room, the nurse flipped on half of the lights. Tables and chairs filled Bess's view but nothing else. Bess stepped into the dimly lit room.

"I don't see anyone," the nurse said, turning to Bess. "Are you sure she's in here?"

"Olive?" Bess called out.

There was a few seconds without any response. It was just enough time to cause Bess to question whether she had made a wise choice in encouraging Olive to go off without her. Bess could feel the nurse's eyes glaring at her while she waited for Olive to answer.

"Olive?" Bess called out again.

"I found him," Olive weakly replied from the shadows that were gathered in the back of the dining room.

Bess took a few more steps around the room, but she could only see empty tables and chairs.

"Where are you, Olive?" Bess asked.

"Over here, Bess. I found him. I found Francis," Olive softly answered.

Bess and the nurse quickly made their way across the dining room towards the doors that led into the kitchen. Bess pushed open the kitchen doors and stopped. There on the kitchen floor, Bess could see Olive, her legs curled beneath her, slumped against a refrigerator. It was hard to see in the shadows, but it appeared to Bess that Olive was cradling something in her hands and leaning over it. Olive looked up at Bess and the light from the dining room caught a wide smile. If there was a picture of joy, it was certainly on display on Olive's face. Olive looked back down at her hands, which were obscured by the shadows.

"I thought I lost you, Francis," Olive said.

Bess stepped closer to get a better look at Francis the cat. When she did, she looked into the shadows to find Olive's two hands cupped together. It appeared to Bess that the only thing she was holding was not a cat, but the air.

"Where is Francis?" Bess asked.

"Right here," Olive grinned, raising her cupped hands in the air for Bess to see. "Isn't he just the prettiest cat you've ever seen?"

Bess merely stood with her mouth hanging open. She managed to nod her head just a little. She looked at the expression on the young nurse's face. Her eyes were wide and her mouth was also hanging open. The nurse turned to Bess but no words came out of her mouth. Bess reached down, gently grabbed Olive by the arm and helped her to her feet.

"Well, that was enough excitement for one night," Bess managed to say. "Let's take you and Francis back to your room."

Together the nurse, Bess and Olive walked out of the dining room and down the halls. When they reached Olive's room, the nurse followed Olive and Bess inside. Bess sat on the bed with Olive, while the nurse called another nurse on the phone and reported what had happened. Bess sat on her bed staring down at her empty hands.

"Would you like to hold him?" Olive asked, holding her hands out for Bess to see.

"No," Bess whispered. "I think Francis is quite at home with you, Olive."

Olive merely sat and stared at her hands. While Bess watched Olive smile at her hands, Bess couldn't help but think that this was by far the saddest end to any of her investigations.

HOW TO CATCH A CHET

Bess thought about Olive's situation for the better part of a week. What bothered her most about her latest investigation wasn't Olive's condition, which was sad in itself. What concerned Bess was how old age had taken a toll on Olive's mind. While she tried not to think about it too much, Bess's worst fear was letting old age turn her mind into mush. She'd seen it happen to other residents. Once in a while she even wandered over to the Dementia Unit of Honey Hills and peeked in through the windows at the handful of patients there. Most days, Bess would find them parked in wheelchairs, staring at a television, unaware of their surroundings or the fact that the channel hadn't been changed all day. It was a fate Bess didn't want to meet as she grew older. Olive's situation only made Bess think about this possibility even more. It also made her appreciate her sharp mind and her instincts for people.

So when the morning came for the Waltzing Club to meet, Bess was more than ready to attend. Fun music and dancing was just what she needed to pick up her spirits. However, her hopes for a fun meeting were quickly dashed by Lillian Peck and her two helpless feet. On more than one occasion Chet had to stop dancing with Bess to help Lillian. At the conclusion of the meeting, Bess finally decided to approach Lillian after most of the other members had left. She found Lillian sitting in a chair rubbing her feet and smiling at the members who were leaving.

Bess pulled up a chair and sat down beside her.

"My dear," Bess began, settling into her chair and turning to get a better look at Lillian. "I thought we might stay after for a little while longer. Since you've been having so much trouble with that new step...I thought you might like to practice a bit. I'd be more than happy to help you."

"Thank you, Bess," Lillian smiled. "I think Chet has been enough help for me today."

"Yes," Bess smiled, shifting in her chair next to Lillian. "I've noticed that you've been asking for Chet's help at almost every meeting. I thought I might take some of the burden off of Chet by offering to help you after our meetings."

"How sweet," Lillian grinned as she slipped on her shoes. "That was so thoughtful of you to offer, Bess, but I don't think it will be necessary. I quite enjoy dancing with Chet and I think he enjoys dancing with me. I don't think I'm...a burden."

Bess could feel her face grow flushed after these words. She felt the urge to stake some kind of claim to Chet. However, Chet wasn't hers to claim, and Bess knew it. Lillian had as much a right to dance with him as Bess, which was an uncomfortable fact for Bess to swallow.

She watched as Lillian turned in her seat, leaned close to Bess and waved her closer.

"Let me tell you something about men," Lillian said, reaching over and giving Bess's hand a playful squeeze with her own. "You have plain features with an above average smile, Bess. If I were you, I'd be smiling as much as I could to catch a man. Your smile is your best feature, you know."

"Catch a man?" Bess laughed. "Is that what we do to men....catch them?"

"I don't know about you," Lillian began. "I grew up in a small town where there were a large number of attractive women and a dwindling number of young men. If you needed a date for a dance, you had to catch a man to take you."

"And how did you...catch...your men?" Bess asked.

"I've always found that acting a bit...what words do I want to use...a bit in need of help has always worked for me," Lillian smiled.

"I think the word is "helpless," my dear," Bess observed.

"There is a difference," Lillian said, raising her index finger in the air. "Being helpless means you *require* attention. I don't require attention from Chet...I simply give him a purpose to spend time with me. Men by their very nature like to help. They need to feel wanted. If you can give them that sense of purpose by creating moments when they can resolve a problem...I find most men just feel better about themselves."

"I was married," Bess stated. "I didn't have to *catch* my husband."

"I've been married three times," Lillian countered. "If there's one thing I've learned about men it's that they like to feel important. They like to feel needed. They are drawn to a woman who makes them feel that way. If you're too independent, too headstrong...most men will feel they aren't needed. This is what I've learned from my marriages."

Bess smiled and quietly nodded out of respect for Lillian's well meaning lesson on men.

It seemed odd to Bess that a woman who had so many failed marriages felt qualified to offer such advice. However, Lillian was merely doing what most residents at Honey Hills like to do. Most residents tended to share what they learned from a full life. Lillian was simply doing the same thing.

"Good day, Lillian," Bess said before standing up and leaving the room.

As she walked down the hallway, Bess realized that her worst fears were confirmed. She really did have a rival for Chet's heart. Now she knew Lillian was using her two left feet to catch Chet like he was some kind of fish. Bess just didn't know if Chet would bite or not. She thought about the problem for the rest of the day and hoped that a good night's sleep would wash her concerns away.

BETTER THAN SUNSHINE

When she woke the next morning, there was something different in the air. She could sense it when she got out of bed. She thought about it as she got dressed, fixed her hair, and prepared for another day at the Honey Hills Retirement Center. While she found the sunlight that poured through her window every morning to be warm and soothing, what Bess smelled in the air was better than any ray of sunshine. The morning sun didn't cause her to smile in such a genuine, almost uncontrollable way. The morning sun didn't smell this good.

As she left her room and stepped into the hallway, Bess found the warm smell of baking bread to be stronger than it was in her room. Walking down the hallway, the aroma caused another broad smile to fill her face. It was the kind of smile that she simply couldn't contain. Bess looked around and could tell she was not alone in her sentiments.

Following the flow of people to the dining room, Bess could sense a difference in her fellow residents. Their faces did not bare the same stoic expressions of starting another day of routine. Instead, smiles rode on their lips. Their eyes appeared a bit wider. Even their steps had more energy. Yes, Bess thought, there was something different about this morning. Something warm and welcoming was definitely in the air. It appeared to be the topic of much discussion as everyone headed towards the entrance to the dining room for breakfast.

"What *is* that wonderful aroma?" Bess asked Alma Crisp, whom she spotted in the hallway. Alma, who was usually impeccably dressed, appeared to have hastily thrown on a pair of blue slacks and a gray top. The dull colors just didn't seem to fit Alma, who usually wore clothes with brighter tones.

"Haven't you heard?" Alma asked with a grin. "Chef Frank has quit. There's a new chef in the kitchen. He's a young man who just graduated from Grantham College's culinary program. I believe his name is Tony. It smells like he's made something quite good. That's why I was a bit rushed to get dressed this morning. The smell just made me too hungry."

Bess and Alma followed the line of residents slowly filing into the dining room. Once in the dining room, the smell of warm bread grew richer.

"Smells like cookies," Alma giggled.

"I think it smells like muffins," Bess grinned.

When Bess reached her table, she looked around to see other ladies in the room beaming and nodding at the pleasant aroma filling the air. For the first time in months, Bess observed, there was a genuine buzz of conversation and excitement in the dining room. Without even setting foot in the room, Bess thought, this new young chef had reinvigorated every resident of the Honey Hills Center.

Suddenly the doors to the kitchen burst open, and the Dining Room servers emerged pushing carts. Each cart carried dishes that were piled high with freshly baked croissants. As a cart moved by the table where Bess was seated, she took a deep breath and caught a whiff of the pastries that were about to be served. Now the room was buzzing with laughter and excited conversation.

"If I knew we'd be having such a fancy breakfast, I would have taken my time this morning and dressed up!" Alma laughed from another table.

In a matter of moments, a plate of freshly baked croissants was placed at the center of Bess's table. She watched a slender veil of steam rise up from the croissants and slowly turn in the air. Bess quickly grabbed the plate, took a croissant, and passed the plate to the woman beside her. Bess held the croissant in her hands, inhaled the scent one last time, then moved the pastry to her lips and took a small bite. A perfect blend of bread and butter melted on her tongue, causing Bess to laugh just a little. A hush spread across the room as everyone indulged in what had wetted their appetites for hours.

It was a little thing, Bess thought. Yet, it was always life's little surprises that made a difference in a day. This morning, life was made a little better for most everyone in the dining room because of these small croissants. Bess turned the pasty in her hand and marveled at how something so small could make a morning at the Honey Hills Center a little brighter. Bess savored the taste and took small bites in an attempt to make the magic last. She made it last for a good two minutes…and then her croissant was gone. As she chewed her last bite she watched the servers emerge from the kitchen with carts full of cereal, juice, and milk.

Bess could feel the smile fade from her face. The excitement of the morning was gone. Breakfast, as every resident knew it, was about to commence with the usual choices.

Bess glared at the carts and drew in a deep breath. She wanted to savor the experience for a few more seconds. She wanted to savor the novelty of starting her morning off in a new and different way before returning to her normal routine of oatmeal, juice, and a banana. A few seconds later her oatmeal had been served. Order had been restored. A sense of normalcy had been returned to the Honey Hills Retirement Center.

A MORNING CONSTITUTION

A good walk in the morning is like a handshake to a new day.

These were the words that Bess Bullock was raised on. It was a simple proverb spoken by her father about the value of morning constitutions. It was also a proverb that Bess took to heart. When she was a child, her father was very active. He liked to exercise and enjoyed starting every day with a good walk. It was the same path every day, rain or shine, five blocks into their hometown of Venton and five blocks back home.

As she grew older, Bess marveled at how little variation her father made in his morning walks. It was the same route for most of his life. On the rare occasions when Bess was awake early in the morning, she would join her father for his walks. Once in the town of Venton, she recalled how her father stopped and talked with friends and familiar faces along his route. Many years later, when she walked with a much older version of her father, Bess realized that it wasn't the scenery that he was enjoying on these walks. Nor did he care about the exercise he'd gotten by the end of the walk. It seemed to Bess that what he enjoyed most about his morning walks was the journey. The things he saw. The people he met. Bess was reminded of this because she was now finding herself faced with a similar situation. Unlike her father, she was restless for a change in her morning walks.

When she first moved to the Honey Hills Center, Bess enjoyed stepping out in the mornings and taking a good brisk stroll around the Honey Hills's grounds. Every road, every street, every yard was new to her and she always found something interesting to observe. Unlike her father, Bess varied the paths that she took during her strolls around the Honey Hills grounds. The variation helped to keep her walks fresh and interesting.

As she began her second year of living at the Honey Hills Center, Bess found herself growing weary of taking the same routes in the mornings. She felt like she had covered every inch of the Honey Hills grounds and longed for more. Now that spring was here, brushing most living things with a fine stroke of green, Bess was ready to walk beyond the grounds of the Honey Hills Center. Over the winter she had grown anxious to explore the neighborhood that lay on the other side of the street. She hoped to find new people to meet and new things to see. Now that spring had arrived, she was ready to act on her ambition.

This morning, her notion for a new walking path was especially enticing. The crisp air filled her lungs. The warming sun danced in her eyes. The birds chirped from trees that held bright green buds. The signs of the morning told Bess that winter had finally subsided. It appeared that spring had taken a firm grasp on the day and would will in the warmer weather. Bess turned to the neighborhood that sat across the street from the grounds of the Honey Hills Center. She smiled to herself and began to walk through the parking lot and down the narrow driveway that wound to the street.

Once at the street, she looked both ways, before crossing. It was a little thing to do, merely crossing a street. Yet, when Bess reached the other side and stepped up on the sidewalk she turned to look back at the Honey Hills Center. Standing on the other side of the street, it gave Bess some perspective on the large red brick building that had been her home for the past year. It was a pleasant enough place, Bess thought, but it felt good to get out and see the world beyond the red brick walls of Honey Hills. She turned and looked at an uneven sidewalk that wound around a corner and under some low hanging tree branches. Her eyes followed the sidewalk and then looked up at the homes next to where she was standing.

"Here we go," Bess told herself.

Her eyes glided from side to side while she walked. The sounds of birds would occasionally echo from a nearby tree. Unlike the homes on the grounds of the Honey Hills Center, these houses had backyards that looked lived in. She walked by one yard with children's toys scattered all around the grass. Another yard found a rather large black dog chained to a tree. The dog stood under the shade of the tree, panting, while he watched Bess walk by. She smiled at the dog, whose large pink tongue hung out and dripped on the grass. She also spied a large dish of water for the dog to drink from.

Bess paused at a street corner and smiled at the sound of children's laughter echoing from an adjoining street. Walking by another yard, she could smell freshly cut grass lingering in the air. Her eyes also enjoyed how each home looked different. All the homes on the Honey Hills grounds were single level ranch homes. The construction and appearance of the homes were very similar. The homes she was now looking at along this street varied in size and appearance.

As her eyes moved and her mind soaked in the new images, Bess decided that this would be a fine path to take her morning walks with Chet. It was a path that even her father would have liked, Bess thought.

As she rounded a corner, Bess spotted a figure walking up the street towards her. It appeared to be a man about two blocks away. While his face was not close enough to recognize, Bess could see that the man was overweight, wore dark pants and a long-sleeved white dress shirt. Bess thought that the man appeared to be a bit overdressed to be walking for exercise on such a warm morning. Most people who dressed this nicely, Bess thought, were at work. Yet, this man appeared to be taking a stroll in dress pants and a button down dress shirt.

As they drew closer to each other, Bess was beginning to recognize the man from about one block away. For a split second, she heard a name slip out of her lips.

"Willie?"

The moment she spoke the name, she watched as the heavy set man picked up his pace and quickly turned a corner about a block in front of Bess. She picked up her pace to try to catch him. When Bess reached the corner, the man was nowhere to be found. She stood at the corner and looked up and down the street. It appeared that he had vanished into thin air. Bess wanted to know why.

THE VOLUNTEER

It was generally known that the most valuable person at the Honey Hills Center was not an employee, but a volunteer. From sun up to sun down, William Nagel, "Willie" to everyone who knew him, spent most days roaming the halls, offering to help both residents and nurses with various tasks. Willie was a large, round man prone to wearing the same white shirt and black pants every day. His skin was milky white and his physique was such that only the belt of his pants helped Bess to recognize where his stomach ended and his legs began. His eyes were small and black and reminded Bess of the kind of eyes she'd seen on a duck. Bess saw plenty of ducks in her day since her late husband enjoyed hunting them. Willie also had a smile that was always at the ready, which put most residents at ease when he was around. In short, Willie Nagle was a walking right hand for anyone who needed help. He was universally appreciated and loved by both residents and nurses.

Yet, as was usually the case for Bess, her instincts refused to allow her to share the same admiration for Willie. Her years of work as the only female police officer in her hometown of Venton left Bess with good instincts for people, and a keen knack for observation. While she found them to be invaluable as a police officer, Bess was starting to find her instincts a bit bothersome now that she was in her retirement years.

There were days when she longed to look at someone and take them for face value. However, her instincts would not permit her such a luxury. Every face she looked at was a quick study for her instincts. It was like there was a camera in her brain that would take a snapshot of someone before drawing conclusions about that person in the span of a few seconds. It was not the result of conscious thought, Bess told herself. It was instinct. She simply had a natural ability to read people. For Bess, it was something as natural as breathing or blinking. It was also something she couldn't control.

She normally saw Willie around dinner time. That was when she would sit and watch Willie help the employees serve dinner in the dining hall. Of course there was nothing wrong with how he served the food, smiling and greeting each resident he handed a plate to. No, what Bess found odd was something that she observed one evening in the dining hall.

After most dinners, Bess was usually the last person at her table where she enjoyed her coffee. It gave her time to reflect on the conversations she'd just enjoyed with the other ladies who sat with her. It also gave her some time to think about the day to come, and to identify one thing she would look forward to about that day. Of course, finding things to look forward to in a retirement home was sometimes a bit of a challenge. Bess saw it as an intellectual exercise. It was the kind of mental task that required her to do a good bit of thinking before identifying that one special thing that would arrive with the coming day.

One evening, Bess found herself alone in the dining hall. She was sitting at her table, sipping warm coffee, reflecting on her meal and the events of the day. In between thoughts, Bess looked around to see Willie Nagle quietly picking up dirty dishes from various tables and carrying them into the kitchen. While sipping her coffee, her eyes followed Willie from the dining hall to the kitchen and back again. On one trip into the kitchen she saw him suddenly pause in the doorway. Bess wondered if he was okay. She watched him stand in the doorway staring down at a plate in his hand. It was at this moment that Bess saw something incredible. She watched as Willie looked over his shoulder to the nearly empty dining room. Suddenly, he plucked a leftover grilled cheese sandwich from a dirty dish and stuck the entire sandwich in his mouth. His cheeks puffed out like a squirrel and he quickly chewed up the sandwich in a matter of seconds.

"Oh my," Bess said to herself.

She'd never seen anything like it. She didn't know which was more shocking, the fact that this man had devoured an entire sandwich in one bite, or that he had done so despite the fact someone else had handled the sandwich and perhaps taken a few small bites from it. She watched Willie's head snap from side to side, as if checking for any bystanders. Bess quickly directed her eyes down to her coffee so as not to meet his glance. After a few seconds, she could hear dishes being clanked and looked up to find that Willie had resumed his duties of clearing dirty dishes and glasses from the tables.

For the rest of the week after dinner, Bess would linger over her coffee and watch Willie carry the dishes from the tables to the kitchen. Every so often she'd spot him snatch a few chips from a plate and pop them into his mouth. On one other occasion, she saw him linger in the doorway between the kitchen and the dining hall. This time he proceeded to stick not one but two dinner rolls in his mouth at the same time. Leftover food on a discarded plate just didn't seem to be safe around Willie Nagel. Bess wanted to know why.

A CHANGE ON TUESDAY MORNINGS

When she worked as the only female police officer in her hometown of Venton, Bess Bullock looked forward to Saturdays the most. After a week of maintaining some type of order in the neighborhood where she patrolled as a police officer, Bess enjoyed spending a full day trying to create a similar sense of order in her home. From the moment she woke, Bess would think about all the jobs that needed to be done around the house. The day usually began by ridding herself of the piles of clothes that needed to be washed. In between loads of laundry, she'd manage to dust the rooms that required attention. Cleaning the bathrooms was also a necessity, as was picking up the usual scattering of toys and clothes spread along Samantha's bedroom floor. Bess would take a break for lunch before sweeping the floors. There was always so much to be done as a young mother, and Saturday was always the best day for Bess to do it all.

Now in her retirement years, and living in the Honey Hills Center, there were people who came around to her room to do the cleaning and the dusting. There were even people to do her laundry. Saturday just wasn't as special for Bess as it once had been. Now her new favorite day of the week was Tuesday. However, this favorite day did not require her to dust and clean. This was the day she got out of her routine and enjoyed the company of good friends and cards.

As she rounded the corner to meet her friends, Bess could feel a smile creeping across her face. When she arrived at the game room, Bess expected to be greeted by the familiar sight of her friends sitting around a table preparing to deal cards. Instead she saw something completely different. Something that wiped away the smile from her lips.

"What have we here?" Bess asked herself.

Instead of being greeted by the sight of her friends seated around a table engaged in conversation and cards, Bess saw that the game room's lights were dimmed. Her friends were gathered around a door that she guessed was locked. Alma Crisp was the first one to look at Bess. Alma was one of the Honey Hills Center's sharpest dressers. This morning she chose to arrive to play cards wearing bright yellow slacks with a white blouse and a matching yellow scarf tied around her neck. Alma turned and made her way over to Bess.

"I don't think we'll be playing cards this morning," Alma sighed.

Bess walked up to where Flo and Rose were standing. Together they stood and stared at the bright orange sign posted on the door to the game room.

"Under construction," Bess said, reading the sign out loud.

She stepped up to the glass and peered inside the game room. There Bess saw the most unfamiliar image of two young men, dressed in blue jeans and t-shirts, moving the table where Bess and her friends usually played Bridge. She scanned the floor where she saw tool boxes, a long orange extension cord, a dull white tarp, and a ladder laying on its side. Bess turned her eyes back to her friends.

"What are they doing in there?" Bess asked.

"The one young man in there told me the whole story," Rose reported. "Seems a pipe broke and flooded our game room last night. He told me we wouldn't be able to go in there for quite some time. He said he needed to pull up the rug, dry the floor, air out the room and make certain there wouldn't be any mold left over. He said it could take a month."

"A month?" Bess said, turning her eyes back to the room. There were so many good memories about that table and that room. Though Bess had only lived here for just over a year, she enjoyed playing cards with her friends every week. The idea of not playing cards caused her heart to race. She looked at the concerned faces of her friends.

"Do we want to take a one month break, ladies?" Bess asked.

"I for one like our card games," Flo Morganstern spoke up. Flo was the most competitive member of the group. Bess thought it would also be hard for Flo not to play cards. While Bess enjoyed it for the social aspects, Flo came for the competition. "I don't want us to stop playing."

"I agree," Alma replied. As the newest member of the group, Alma was just beginning to enjoy the routine and the socializing, Bess thought. "I would also like to keep playing."

"Me too," Rose nodded. The oldest member of the group, Rose had lived at the Honey Hills Center longer than anyone else in the group. "Bess? I can only guess...but would you like to continue with our group?"

"Of course," Bess answered. "You're my friends. Whoever heard of taking a break from friendship...even if it is over cards."

"Very well," Rose nodded. "Then I'd suppose we'll need a new room to play cards in. We all know how small our rooms are. Four ladies meeting in one of our rooms just wouldn't be possible. Any other ideas come to mind?"

"How about the dining hall?" Alma asked. "We could ignore the smell of the food to play. We could meet in the dining room between breakfast and lunch."

"Yes," Rose nodded, "I'm afraid they lock the doors when they aren't serving meals, though. Perhaps I could speak to someone about that idea."

"There's a large table down in the west wing of the center," Bess spoke up. It's a table surrounded by six chairs. We could go there."

"Too drafty," Flo grumbled. "I know where that table is and there are two large vents in the ceiling. I don't want to bring my sweater with me every time we play cards. I don't want to catch a cold in the summer, either."

"So where can we play?" Bess asked.

"How about the book room?" Alma suggested. "They've got a long table. There are enough chairs for everyone. No drafts that I can think of. It's quiet...so we should be able to concentrate on our Bridge games."

"The book room," Rose said, a smile slowly rising on her face. "Of course! They never lock that door. The book room is always open. My book group meets in the evening so the mornings should be free"

"Let's go down right now," Bess suggested, waving the other ladies down the hallway.

In a few minutes, they entered a long narrow room filled with dull red carpeting. At the corners of the room were large cushioned chairs placed next to lights and windows. Along the walls were shelves packed with paperback books and magazines. In the center of the room, a table with neatly folded newspapers on it. Bess had been in this room many times. She tried to read one book a week, but her investigations were cutting into that goal. Each time she was in the room, browsing for a title to consider, she could not recall one occasion where she saw someone reading the newspapers.

"Let's play," Flo said, quickly sitting down and shuffling the cards in her hand.

Silence followed for the next few minutes. Bess watched the cards slide across the smooth wood table top. She had to move her hand quickly to catch some of the cards that skimmed across the polished surface. After receiving her final card, Bess examined her hand, looked around, and decided to present a question for conversation.

"Do any of you know Willie Nagel?" she asked.

"Of course," Rose quickly answered. "Everyone knows Willie. He practically lives here. He volunteers all the time."

"He helped me hang a picture in my room the other day," Flo announced from behind her cards. "It's nice having a man around to help out like that. I told him he's our rooster in the hen house....since he helps all us women. He thought that was funny."

"I've seen him in the hallway," Alma said. "I haven't really spoken to him. We've just exchanged smiles."

"There's something about him," Bess sighed. She paused for a moment, bit her bottom lip, and could still feel her instincts stir when the image of Willie flashed in her mind. "I can't quite put my finger on it. Like you, Rose, I do see him here quite a bit. In fact, I see him more than any other volunteer at Honey Hills. Yes, he is very helpful with things, Flo. I have also exchanged smiles with him, Alma. He does seem very pleasant...but..."

"But what?" Rose asked.

"Well...I don't know how to phrase this...for the last week I've seen him eating left over food after dinner in the dining room," Bess stated.

"What sort of food?" Flo asked.

"The first time I saw him, he ate an entire grilled cheese sandwich," Bess replied. "His cheeks puffed out like a fish. Another time I saw him pop two left over dinner rolls in his mouth and swallow them like they were pills. I swear he only chewed twice before he swallowed those rolls. It really was quite a sight."

"He's a large man," Flo sighed, adjusting the cards in her hand. "He could be hungry."

"Yes, that could be it," Rose chimed in.

"Perhaps he's trying some kind of diet," Alma suggested. She lowered her cards from her face, shook her head and smiled. "You know when I'm on a diet...sometimes I feel like I could eat a horse at the end of the day."

"I can understand being hungry," Bess said, lowering her cards and pointing across the table at Alma. "It would have been one thing if he stood there and took small bites and finished that sandwich like a normal person would. I just thought it was odd the way he stood to the side, looked around, and quickly swallowed those table scraps the way he did. It just reminded me of something...but I'm not quite sure of what."

"Eating someone else's left over food is unusual," Rose sighed and she followed her comment with a knowing glance around the table. "I can understand your suspicions, Bess. However, where is the mystery in a large man like Willie being hungry? While disgusting as it may be...there's no mystery in a large man wanting to eat."

"Maybe you're the one who's hungry, Bess," Flo laughed.

"Excuse me?" Bess asked and she turned in her seat. She steadied her gaze on Flo. Bess wasn't quite sure what Flo was saying and she lowered her cards while she waited for a response to her question.

"What I mean," Flo explained, "is that it's been a while since you've uncovered a mystery to solve. You've been on a dry spell, Bess. Maybe you're looking too hard for something to investigate. That's all I meant...that *you're* hungry for a mystery. I certainly didn't mean you were fat...like Willie. I mean, look at you. The wind could pretty much knock you over. You're such a petite thing, I still can't believe you used to be a police officer."

Bess smiled as she listened to Flo fumble with her words to explain her comment. A quiet game of cards followed and as they played their hands, Bess began to think about Willie again. What would drive someone to eat table scraps? Was it simply hunger? Was there something more to it? The longer she thought about it, the more Bess could feel her investigative instincts begin to drive her mind. There was something more to it, Bess thought.

She trusted her instincts and wondered where they would take her in the investigation of Willie Nagel.

CLUES OVER CROISSANTS

One evening Bess sat quietly at the end of her meal. She had just finished a plate of spaghetti with a very spicy marinara sauce, which Bess found delightful. She also enjoyed a slice of homemade garlic bread that she hated to finish. The butter and garlic melted in her mouth like the croissant she enjoyed for breakfast. Whoever Chef Tony was, Bess thought, his skills as a cook were making everyone forget about the dull tasting meals once made by Chef Frank. Once done with her garlic bread, Bess remained in the dining hall while the other ladies left. She was the last one in the room taking sips of her coffee while she watched Willie clear away dirty dishes from each table.

As she observed him move between the dining room and the kitchen, Bess was relieved to see that Willie was not going to eat leftover spaghetti or garlic bread crusts. She watched him clear one table, load the dirty dishes onto a cart, and then push the cart into the kitchen before returning for more dishes. When he got close to the table where Bess was seated, his head turned and his eyes locked on Bess. He smiled and made his way over to where she was seated.

"All done, Mrs. Bullock?" Willie asked, reaching for her dish.

"Yes, thank you," Bess answered. She handed him her plate and spotted some tomato sauce that had smeared along the cuff of his rolled up white shirt sleeve. It looked like someone took a paint marker and made a small narrow streak of red. She tried not to draw attention to it and smiled at Willie.

"You certainly work quite hard, Willie," Bess observed.

"If you like what you do," Willie explained, "it isn't work."

"I've been thinking about you, Willie," Bess announced and she put her coffee mug down. "I have a shelf in my room that I'd like to move. I realize that it's late...perhaps you could come by my room tomorrow morning and help me with it. If it wouldn't be too much trouble."

"No request is ever a problem, Mrs. Bullock," Willie replied. "I'd be happy to stop by tomorrow."

"Shall we say...after breakfast?" Bess asked.

"Right after I'm done helping in the dining room," Willie replied.

Bess smiled at the comment and took one final sip of her coffee before getting up to leave.

The next morning, Bess arrived in her room right after another delightful breakfast of warm croissants, cereal and juice. Bess left the door open, sat in her chair, and waited for her guest to arrive. Ten minutes later, as promised, Willie appeared in the doorway.

"Good morning, Bess," Willie said, stepping into the room with his trade mark black pants and white shirt.

"Thank you for coming, Willie," Bess said with a smile. She pointed across the room at a three foot high wood shelf. Bess had carefully removed the books from the shelf the previous night. She wanted it to go along a wall that got more daylight so she could better read the titles on the binding.

"That doesn't look like too much trouble," Willie announced. He walked across the room, wrapped his hefty arms around the shelf, and made a sound like he was clearing his throat before lifting it.   He slowly turned and moved across the room to a spot located along a wall where Bess was standing.   When he finished, his face had grown pink from the exertion.

"My, you are strong," Bess smiled and gestured to a chair. "Please, sit down, Willie. I have something to thank you for your help."

Willie quickly responded to the offer, letting a puff of air escape from his plump cheeks before dropping into the chair.   Bess quietly opened her closet door and pulled out a brown paper bag.   She carried the paper bag to her chair and stopped in front of Willie.   She dipped her hands into the bag and pulled out a small cardboard box.   A sweet aroma accompanied the box and she noticed how Willie's eyes lit up.   She handed him the box without hesitation.

"I think there are a dozen croissants in there," Bess smiled. "I picked them up this morning.   Tony the chef had some extra ones and he was kind enough to give them to me.   I told him they were for you.   He said you worked too hard and that you deserved them."

"Mrs. Bullock," Willie smiled, running his hand across the lid of the box. "That was very kind of you."

"Please," Bess said, gesturing to the box.   "Go ahead and help yourself."

She watched as Willie's dark eyes turned down to the box he was cradling on his round stomach.   He quickly opened the lid, grabbed the first unsuspecting croissant and popped the whole thing in his mouth. Bess gasped for a second, then caught herself and tried to keep a sense of calm on her face.   She watched as Willie devoured another croissant, followed by another and another.   As he ate, Bess found her eyes riding along the long sleeved white dress shirt that he was wearing.   Her eyes scanned his one sleeve and then stopped. There along the cuff of his shirt she noted a tomato sauce stain on the cuff. Her eyes narrowed and she looked up at the heavy set man feasting on croissants in her room.

For most people, a change of clothes would be a requirement each day. She had known people who didn't adhere to such a norm. Many years ago, she knew people who wore the same clothes every day. As she looked at Willie's black pants and white shirt with the stain on the sleeve, she suspected there was more to Willie than a healthy appetite. What she was looking at was a vaguely familiar picture. A picture she'd seen before and suspected had emerged in her life again.

"Mr. Nagel," Bess began, leaning in a little closer. "Perhaps you didn't know it, but I was a former police officer in the town of Venton. I had a part of the city to walk every day and I'd see the same people every day. It was a nice way to get to know the community. I got to know everyone from business leaders to school kids when I did my patrol."

"Really, Mrs. Bullock?" Willie managed to say before cramming another croissant in his mouth.

"I also got to know the homeless people who lived in some of the poor sections of Venton," Bess continued. "I found homeless people to be very nice. They were just people who had a bit of bad luck. A lost job. A factory closed. A house that burned down. There was always a reason behind their misfortune."

She looked at Willie, who had stopped eating the croissants. His eyes were now turned down to the floor. He was no longer smiling. He wasn't even looking at her.

"I remember how they wore the same clothes for days at a time," Bess continued, eyeing up his ever present black pants and white shirt.

"Sometimes I'd give them food," Bess continued. "I'd buy an apple or a peach from the market vendor and give it to a homeless person. Watching a homeless person eat is just something I'll never forget, Willie. The way they'd grip the food, the quick snaps of the teeth, the fast chewing motion, it was like watching a hungry animal devour something. I find myself thinking about that experience when I watch you in the dining hall. I've seen the way you eat leftover food from other people's plates. You eat with the same vigor."

Her words caused his eyes to look up at her. His mouth hung open and his eyes were now locked on her. She thought it interesting that he didn't object to what she was saying. He wasn't going to defend himself against her suspicions.

"I also notice that you're wearing the same shirt from yesterday," Bess said. She pointed to the cuff of his shirt. "You got a spaghetti sauce stain there on your sleeve when you were clearing the tables in the dining hall yesterday. Of course, I didn't want to draw attention to it. I didn't want to embarrass you…so I chose not to say anything. However, I can still see it this morning. I know it's a small thing, and one would have to get quite close to notice it, but there it is."

Willie quietly nodded without making eye contact with Bess.

"So tell me," Bess said, leaning forward in her seat. She gave him a small smile and in the softest tone of voice she could muster asked one simple question. "Please, Willie, tell me what happened to you?"

WILLIE'S PLIGHT

"As you know," Willie began. "I am a bachelor. I lived in the home I was raised in. Both of my parents have passed away, so I live pretty much by myself. There were lots of good things about leading a bachelor's life. I could eat what I wanted and when I wanted. I could dress any way I wanted and I didn't have to worry about what my parents would say. If I was hot in the winter and I'd put on a pair of shorts to walk around the house, no one would tell me otherwise. I could stay up late, watch TV, and fall asleep on my sofa if I wanted to. I enjoyed living in my house as a bachelor. It was a good life, even after my parents died," Willie explained.

"Being a bachelor sounds like a fun life to me," Bess smiled. "I can't help but notice that you keep using the past tense when you talk about these things, Willie."

Willie slowly nodded in reply to her words.

"There was one day…when I came here to volunteer," Willie began. He cleared his throat and picked at something on his pants leg. "I was in a hurry to leave the house that morning. Of course, you know I love coming here. I enjoy talking to the people. They make me feel…valued. I like that. It's a feeling you don't get too much when you're a bachelor living by yourself."

"I think I understand what you mean," Bess mumbled to herself, thinking of some of her experiences as a Honey Hills resident. There were days when she felt just as isolated and just as starved for a compliment from someone.

"That was why I left my house in such a hurry that one morning. I couldn't wait to get here," Willie continued. He looked down at the floor and sighed. "So on that morning I was up early, I had my morning coffee and I got dressed to come here. You see, I got laid off from my job which is why I volunteer here. The factory where I worked sent more jobs to other countries and shut down. I am not a young man, Mrs. Bullock, as you can tell. It is harder than I thought it would be to find work again. The Honey Hills Center was the only place I could come to while I waited for another job to come through. Unfortunately, that one morning I was telling you about...that one morning when I had my morning coffee...I left the house with the coffee maker running. Being a bachelor, there was no one in the house to unplug it for me. While I came here that morning to help the residents of the Honey Hills Center, my house was burning to the ground. The fire department told me that the source of the fire began with the coffeemaker."

"A fire?" Bess asked. "So your house is...gone?"

"Yes," Willie whispered. He looked around as if checking to see if any other people were in Bess's room. He looked at her with his small dark eyes. "No house...no job...that's my life right now, Mrs. Bullock. Please don't tell anyone."

"I won't tell," Bess said with a subtle nod. She leaned forward a bit. "It might be something that *you* should talk about, Willie."

"What do you mean?" Willie asked and he rubbed his chin before considering her advice.

"As I used to tell the homeless people in Venton," Bess began. "You've had a bad break in your life. Now you need to make a good break. The only way you'll get a good break is if you ask for help. That's what you need to do, Willie. You need to share your news and hope that someone will help you."

"It's not that bad," Willie sighed and his eyes turned out her window. "I stick around here a lot and help out. No one questions me when I'm here, no matter what time of the day or night. I use the restrooms here for occasional sponge baths when it's late and everyone is asleep. Sometimes I catch a few winks in a chair at night. I get up early and help with breakfast...and sneak some food from the dining hall to eat."

"Yes...I noticed that," Bess said with a shake of her head. The image of him eating food that other people had handled made her stomach turn. "So, Willie, when will you be able to stop eating table scraps and start making your own meals? Do you have a plan?"

Bess watched as Willie sat quietly. No words seem to come to him for a reply.

"We need to start by finding you a job, Willie. We need to get you some money. That will be a start," Bess said.

"How can I do that?" Willie asked and she could detect a hint of frustration in his voice. "I have no place to live. No phone for people to call me. No mail address for employers to send me important letters. How will I get a job without a home?"

"It's clear you are a good worker," Bess nodded. "Everyone here can attest to that. I think we should find you a job here that will earn you some money."

"A job...at the Honey Hills Center?" Willie asked. "How can I get a job here?"

It sounded like a mystery to Bess. How could she get a job for a man with no formal education and no home? Years ago she tried to help the homeless in

Venton, but she was younger and not as wise about people's attitudes back then. Now many years older, she had one last chance to help a homeless person. She was determined not to let Willie Nagel down.

THE HOUSE ON DOGWOOD

With the weather growing warmer, and the sun beginning to linger longer in the sky, Bess was able to persuade Chet to go on some walks with her after supper. They had grown quite close over the year since Bess first moved into Honey Hills. Chet even stole a kiss from Bess on her birthday, a gesture she didn't mind in the least. Since that kiss they agreed to find more time to hold hands and talk, besides at Waltzing Club meetings. It was Bess who suggested after dinner walks.

During the winter months, they would stroll around the lengthy hallways of the Honey Hills Center after dinner, chatting with friends and catching up on the latest gossip. Now that the weather was getting warmer, Bess persuaded Chet into moving their evening strolls outdoors. With fewer people to see, Bess quite enjoyed having Chet all to herself. Though the spring air could be brisk some evenings, they simply slipped on coats for some of their walks. If the sun was out, its golden rays gave Chet and Bess enough warmth to take their strolls without coats. It also gave them time to talk about their days. As they neared Dogwood Lane, Bess began to stare at a small house that was for sale. It was a ranch home, one of many homes where some residents lived. They were usually owned by couples who were in good physical shape and didn't need assistance from nurses. While she enjoyed living in the main building of the Honey Hills Center, Bess occasionally found herself dreaming of living in a home again.

"There's your house," Chet said as they turned down Dogwood Lane.

"My house?" Bess laughed, squeezing Chet's hand. "Why would you say that?"

"It's not because of anything you say…but you look at it more than the other homes we pass on our walks," Chet observed.

Her eyes glided over the small red brick ranch home, the small porch and the two large windows that revealed a dark and empty living room. Bess followed Chet down the street to where it turned, then got a good view of her favorite part of the house; the backyard. It was the most interesting part of the property, Bess thought, because of the two massive gardens that were tucked into one corner of the yard.

"There you go again," Chet quietly laughed.

"What?" Bess asked.

"We walk down this street almost every day," Chet said. "I always see your eyes lock on that backyard longer than you look at the house. What is so interesting about that yard?"

"This is where Marge and Harvey Dent used to live," Bess explained. "Marge always had the sweetest smelling rose bushes in her gardens. It really was like having sweet taffy stretched under your nose. Then Harvey came down with some form of dementia and they had to move into the Honey Hills Center for Harvey's safety. It's such a shame to look at her garden now. Two patches of dirt are all that remain from what was once a very beautiful garden. It's just sad…I think."

"Perhaps someone will come along to restore that beauty again," Chet observed.

"One can only hope," Bess replied and she felt a small smile follow her words. She kept her eyes focused on the yard. "An unused garden is like an unused life. All I think about are the lost possibilities of those two gardens."

They began to head back to the Honey Hills Center when they walked by another couple taking a walk. The man was tall and lean with a large nose that easily propped up his glasses. The woman was shorter, with a round belly and a slight limp when she walked. Bess offered them wishes for a good day and before she knew it a conversation began to blossom between the couples.

"I'm Bunny Steinman," the woman announced with a cheerful grin. She turned and grabbed the hand of the man beside her. "This is my husband Paul."

"Pleasure to meet you two," Chet replied. "I'm Chet Wooden and this is Bess Bullock."

"Well it's a lovely morning for a walk," Paul Steinman observed. "You two walk a lot?"

"Yes," Bess explained. "We try to get out for walks on mornings like this."

"I don't remember seeing you around here," Bunny said and she rubbed her chin with her finger while she studied Bess's face. "Paul and I are frequent walkers, but I don't recall seeing you two around here. What street do you live on?"

"We don't live on a street," Bess said, her eyes lowering as if she was confessing to some kind of sin. "Chet and I live in the main building of the Honey Hills Center."

"Well, that explains it," Bunny nodded. "So you came out for some fresh air."

"Yes," Bess nodded. She took a step closer to Bunny and Chet. "I've always wondered how nice these homes are to live in. Do you like living in them?"

"Oh yes," Bunny quickly replied. "You see, Paul and I have a home on Evergreen Road. Our house is near a farmer's field. We have a beautiful view of some horses from our kitchen window where we eat breakfast."

"That sounds lovely," Bess smiled.

"We really don't even see the Honey Hills Center from our home, Bunny continued.

"Sometimes I think we both forget that we're living in a retirement community, don't we Paul?"

Paul offered a quiet nod in reply.

"It's like...we're in a nice little neighborhood where everyone is nice and we're all around the same age," Bunny tried to explain. "We wave to each other. We walk over to each other's homes to visit. The Honey Hills Center is close enough to us in case we have any problems...but it's far enough away that we don't see it. Really it's the best of both worlds."

Bess could only smile and nod at the comments. Chet picked up the conversation while Bess began to think about that empty house on Dogwood Lane.

After their walk, Bess and Chet found their way back into the Honey Hills Center. They smiled to each other when the warm air of the center greeted their faces. They removed their coats at the same time, turned down a hallway and then paused in front of the door to Chet's room. Chet turned to Bess and smiled.

"That was a nice couple we talked to," Chet said. "They sounded like they quite enjoyed living in one of those homes. How would you like it?"

"Oh, Chet," Bess sighed and waved her hand. "That is where they belong and in here is where we belong. We each have our lives to lead."

"Life is always about possibilities, Bess," Chet stated. He laughed a little. "If you had your choice...I know you'd rather be working in those gardens than sitting in your room."

"Chet," Bess sighed. She smiled at him and touched the side of his face with her hand. "You're such a dreamer. A dreamer is the best kind of person to share a walk with. Maybe that's why I love our walks together."

"I enjoy our walks, too," Chet replied and he finally let go of Bess's hand. "See you tomorrow morning for dance?"

"Yes," Bess smiled and the face of Lillian flashed in her mind.

Bess cleared her throat and turned down the hallway and began to walk to her room. She took small measured steps and began to think about her predicament with Lillian. While conflict was never her favorite way to go, Bess was beginning to realize that a full confrontation might be in order to get to the root of Lillian's helplessness.

"Mrs. Bullock!" a woman's voice called out.

Bess stopped in the hallway and turned to see a young woman walking briskly down the hallway waving her hand in the air in a gesture to get Bess's attention. Bess watched the young woman step around a slow moving resident and nearly collide with a nurse pushing a cart. The young woman stopped right in front of Bess breathing quite hard.

"Mrs. Bullock! Oh thank heavens I caught you!" the woman gasped in between deep breaths.

"My goodness, dear," Bess said, resting her hand on the young woman's shoulder. "You almost got knocked down by that cart. Why are you in such a hurry? Is something wrong?"

"Mrs. Deb McKenzie sent me for you," the young woman said. "I'm Amanda McKenzie. Deb McKenzie is my mother."

"Oh yes," Bess nodded. "Your mother started a daycare center here at Honey Hills a month ago. I do recall seeing you and her walking the young children around. I must tell you how pleasant it is to hear children's voices laughing in the hallway."

"My mother really needs your help," Amanda puffed and she grabbed Bess by the arm.

Normally, Bess would have pulled her arm away. However, she was curious. Her instincts told her that when a daughter comes running down a hallway looking for someone for her mother it must be important. The way she ignored Bess's compliment towards the children simply reinforced the importance of the request. Bess quickened her pace. The further they walked, the more clearly the voices of children could be heard.

Bess thought back to the dark cold days of winter. It was during the winter season that she found herself making a point of walking by the windows of the Honey Hills Daycare Center.

Bess would linger by the windows and enjoy watching the children. Their energy and enthusiasm always managed to brighten the day for Bess. It was the only hallway in Honey Hills that had constant noise and activity, thus making it one of Bess's favorite hallways to walk through. When Bess followed Amanda through the door to the daycare, the muffled sound of children's voices grew sharper than in the hallway.

"Mom...she's here!" Amanda announced.

Bess looked around at the children swirling around the room. Toys were scattered around her feet and Bess quickly became mindful of where she stepped. One little girl walked up and grabbed hold of Bess by the hand and stood beside her squeezing her thumb. Two boys were building with blocks in one corner. A smaller girl was coloring with crayons at a table.

Two more girls were playing with clay at another table. Bess turned to see an older woman walk up to her. The woman was holding a baby and Bess was fairly certain she knew who the woman was.

"Mrs. McKenzie," Bess smiled. "You certainly do seem to have quite a busy room here."

"We are busy *every* day," Mrs. McKenzie replied, but there was no smile after her words.

"I've heard conversations about you, Mrs. Bullock. Are you the Mrs. Bullock who used to be a police officer? Are you the one who solves mysteries for other residents?"

"Yes, I am," Bess answered.

"How long does it take for you to solve a mystery for someone?" Mrs. McKenzie asked.

"Excuse me?" Bess replied, a bit confused by the question.

"Can you solve mysteries quickly?" Mrs. McKenzie pressed. She folded her arms after asking this question and she leaned her head forward slightly while she waited for Bess to answer. Bess could sense the importance of this question, even though it sounded a bit ridiculous to her.

"Well…I never really timed myself," Bess laughed. "I'd suppose it depends on what the mystery is. Some require more time than others…why?"

"Because I need your help finding something," Mrs. McKenzie explained. She stepped around a little girl playing on the floor and moved closer to Bess. "No one must know about this, Mrs. Bullock. You must not tell anyone. What I'm about to tell you is something that must be resolved in a matter of hours. Do you think you could do that?"

"Tell me more," Bess asked, intrigued by the conditions that were being laid out for this particular investigation.

THE VANISHING BOY

"We are missing a little boy," Mrs. McKenzie reported and she folded her arms, as if hugging herself after the comment. "His name is Jacob. I'd rather not mention his last name...but I can tell you his first name is Jacob."

"So Jacob is...missing?" Bess asked, mindful to soften her voice. "That is quite a serious matter, Mrs. McKenzie. If I may ask...how do you lose a child?"

"Jacob is new to our room," Mrs. McKenzie began, her eyes gliding around the room at the activity and the children. "His mother was recently hired as a nurse at the Honey Hills Center. When she brought him here on Monday, she told us he is prone to wandering off. We promised to keep a good eye on him...and we did for the last few days. I just never thought my promise would be tested so soon."

"When did you notice Jacob was not in the room?" Bess asked.

"We took the children for a walk this morning," Mrs. McKenzie recalled. "You know it is spring time and I thought Amanda and I could take them for a walk around the grounds. We smelled some flowers, spotted some birds, and looked at how the green leaves are coming out on the trees. It was a lovely morning and we all came back safely."

"So Jacob returned from the walk with you?" Bess asked.

"Yes," Mrs. McKenzie replied. "I remember we were all going to sit down at the tables for a snack and a drink after our walk. The children were washing their hands while I was getting snacks together. When all the children were seated, I served their snacks. We had one extra drink and pretzel. I looked around and noticed that Jacob was gone."

"And how long has the boy been missing?" Bess asked.

"About a half hour," Mrs. McKenzie reported. "I sent Amanda over to see if Jacob was with his mother. Children sometimes like to see their parents and since it was his third day with us I only suspected that he went looking for his mother. It wasn't until Amanda came back without Jacob that I knew we had a serious problem. That's when I sent for you, Mrs. Bullock."

"Perhaps you should you contact the police," Bess suggested.

"I don't think any harm has come to him," Mrs. McKenzie replied. "He's a mischievous boy. There are only kind people here at the Honey Hills Center. I think he's just gone exploring."

"If he's still at the Honey Hills Center," Bess stated and she followed her words with a steady gaze. "He may have wondered off the grounds."

"Please, Mrs. Bullock," Mrs. McKenzie said. "Can you try to do something? If you can't find him, I will contact the police and his mother. I just hate to put the mother through so much worry. Like I said...I don't think any harm has come to him."

"I will try to help," Bess nodded. She could tell Mrs. McKenzie was quite concerned, though she was trying not to let her fears show to the other children. "I'd suppose a good place to start would be to know something about Jacob. What does he look like?"

"He's about this tall," Mrs. McKenzie said tapping her hand to her waist. "He has short brown hair, he's wearing a bright green shirt today with blue jeans."

"He likes farms," a voice called out from the floor.

Bess looked down to see a small boy crawling under her legs. The boy was pushing a small metal tractor and he looked up at Bess.

"Jacob plays farm with me," the boy announced. "He's gonna be a farmer when he gets big. He tells me that when we play."

"A farmer," Bess smiled at the boy. "Is that what Jacob says?"

"Yes," answered the boy. He stood up and cradled the tractor in his hands. "We 're gonna have our own farm, me and Jacob."

"Lester," Mrs. McKenzie said, "please go play and let me talk to Mrs. Bullock."

While Mrs. McKenzie spoke with Lester, Bess began to walk around the room. She stepped around some little girls sitting on the floor beside a doll house. She moved around a small table where she peeked over the shoulder of a boy coloring with crayons. Bess continued to weave around the children in the classroom before she stopped in front of a bulletin board. Bess stood quietly and watched Amanda hang up hand drawn pictures of birds, trees, a smiling sun, and lots of other happy pictures celebrating the arrival of spring.

"Those look pretty," Bess said, pointing up to the bulletin board. "Did the children make those?"

"Yes," Amanda answered while she stapled another picture up. "After the walk this morning, Mom had the children make pictures of what they liked the best."

"I see," Bess answered. She stepped a little closer to the bulletin board. Once all the pictures were hung, Bess looked around at the colorful images. Uneven lines of brightly colored flowers, rainbows and butterflies filled her vision. Then, quite suddenly her eyes detected something out of place. She found her eyes locked on one picture. It was the only picture of the group that was not filled with bright colors. Bess reached up with her finger, tapped the picture and turned to Amanda. "What is this?"

"I don't know," Amanda replied. "Jacob made it. He's always doing things differently than the other children."

Bess stood and stared at the picture. It was something brown, shaped like a square with a triangle on top. Beside the square stood a tall rectangle. Bess examined the picture closely, her nose practically touching the paper.

"I know this building," Bess mumbled to herself.

"That's a barn," Lester spoke up. "Jacob said he was drawing a barn."

"Where did Jacob see this barn?" Bess asked.

"On the walk," Lester replied.

"Of course," Bess said. She reached up and yanked the picture off the bulletin board.

"Mrs. Bullock," Mrs. McKenzie stated and she quickly walked across the room. "What are you doing? That's the children's work and they take great pride in it."

"I'm sorry," Bess apologized and folded the paper in half. "May I borrow this?"

"Of course…why?" Mrs. McKenzie asked.

"I think I know where young Jacob might be," Bess announced.

THE MYSTERY OF A BARN

When she stepped outside, Bess squinted up at the sun. It was higher in the sky than it had been when she walked earlier in the morning with Chet. In fact, the sky itself held a brighter blue tint than this morning, almost looking like the shell of a robin's egg. It was also much warmer than a few hours ago. Bess took off her sweater and began to walk along the side of the road that wound around the grounds of the Honey Hills Retirement Center. Few cars drove on the roads, and those that did were expected to travel at fifteen miles per hour, which was clearly posted on more than one sign. She followed the road which led away from the main building and into the independent living development of the Honey Hills Center. Along the sides of the streets, Bess smiled longingly at the small ranch homes that comprised the independent living neighborhood. She was familiar with this walk. It was a stroll she had taken many mornings over the last year where she always found herself looking longingly at the ranch homes and their spacious backyards.

As she walked by the homes, Bess took a deep breath of morning air and tried to stay calm. A missing child was a serious matter. Bess hoped that her instincts were leading her to the right place. She tried to ignore her doubts, given that her conclusions were based on a child's drawing and another child's testimony. Her eyes turned up to the trees where light green leaves were freshly sprouted from branches. Dark green grass had all but replaced the yellowish tint that winter had spread across most yards. A robin chirped from a tree. Bess walked by one yard where she saw a man pulling out weeds from his garden. In another yard, she spotted a woman filling a bird bath with a watering can. The woman spotted Bess and smiled.

"Good morning, Bess!" she called out.

"Good morning!" Bess waved back. "Did you see a young boy during your walk?"

"A young boy?" the woman asked and she shook her head. "Not that I recall."

Bess smiled and thanked her for her response. Moments later Bess spotted another couple that was walking along the opposite side of the street holding hands. When they drew close enough, both husband and wife offered Bess a kind word, which Bess returned with a smile. It was clear to Bess that everyone was quite happy to have the spring season here and quite eager to get out and indulge in the warm weather.

The road stretched out in front of Bess for a few more blocks before it curved to the right. Bess followed the curve and then spotted an old red barn at the end of the street. Bess knew the barn was part of the land that was originally purchased by the Honey Hills Center many years ago. She also knew that the barn was used by the grounds crew to store their equipment. The closer she got to the curve in the road, Bess began to see someone sitting in the grass. It appeared to be a person wearing a bright green shirt. A few steps closer and Bess could see it was a boy who was at the barn at the bottom of the hill. Bess smiled and the pace in her steps began to pick up.

"There he is," Bess whispered and she felt quite relieved after saying those words.

When she approached him, Bess could see his knees were drawn up under his chin. She walked up beside the boy and stopped for a moment.

"Hello," Bess said. She looked down at the boy and thought it would be better if she got down to his level. She tried to slowly lower herself into the grass. Her one knee cracked when she sat, causing the little boy to jump. "What's your name?"

"My name's Jacob," the boy answered.

"Did you make this picture," Bess asked.

She placed her sweater on her lap and held up Jacob's picture of the barn. She handed it to Jacob, who took the picture from her hands and held it in front of his face. He sat quietly staring at his picture and then he smiled.

"It's a barn." he mumbled.

"A very nice barn indeed," Bess said. "My name is Mrs. Bullock. I live at the Honey Hills Center. It's nice to meet you, Jacob. You're a very good artist."

"I remember your name," Jacob said and he turned to look at her. "At dinner time, my mother talks about you, too. She's a nurse…and she says the other nurses tell her you're real smart."

"I guess that's a good thing," Bess nodded, unsure of whether she had just been given a compliment or not. "So why are you sitting out here, Jacob?"

"I'm waiting for the animals," Jacob replied, putting his picture down and pointing out at the barn.

"Animals?" Bess asked. "Are there really animals down there?"

"I think they're in that barn," Jacob replied. "Farmers always keep their animals in a barn. Don't you know that?"

"I guess not," Bess laughed, surprised at the boy's simplistic reasoning. "So you think that's what is in the barn?"

"Yes," Jacob nodded. "The farmer just has to come and let them out. My mom read me a book about barns one time. That's what it said in the book. That's what I'm waiting for."

Bess remained silent for a minute. She rubbed her chin and looked at Jacob. Bess could relate to the strength of his curiosity and the strength of his conviction. Perhaps, Bess thought, this young man would grow up to be a fine police officer in Venton.

"You know, Jacob," Bess began. "This is what I call a mystery. There is something in that barn...but you're not quite sure what it is. You think there are animals in that barn...but you really can't be too sure from looking at it. To solve the mystery, I think we should go down the hill and sneak a peek inside that barn. What do you think?"

"Won't the farmer be angry if we go in the barn?" Jacob asked.

"I don't think so," Bess smiled, and she struggled to her feet. "Sometimes a little investigating is required to solve a mystery, Jacob. That's what we must do."

Together Bess and Jacob made their way down the sloping green grass. When they reached the bottom of the hill, Bess led Jacob to the front doors of the barn. She noticed how the red paint was worn and flaking off the wood exterior. She stopped in front of one of the doors, looked down at Jacob and grinned.

"Aren't mysteries exciting, Jacob?" Bess asked.

Jacob smiled and nodded his head very quickly.

"That's why I like them," Bess stated.

She grabbed hold of a black metal handle, moved a latch, and slid the door open. Soon Bess and Jacob were able to peer inside the barn. Daylight poked through cracks in the walls and ceiling. Shafts of light cut through the darkness. Bess took a few steps into the barn and stopped beside an old tractor that was covered in webs and dust. She felt Jacob's hand slip into her fingers and the feeling of holding a child's hand made her smile.

"Where are the animals?" Jacob asked, his head turning from side to side. "Farmers always keep their animals in barns."

"I don't think this barn has a farmer," Bess explained. "Let's look around."

Together they moved around the barn. Hand in hand, they paused in front of a ride-on lawnmower, some snow blowers, and other types of equipment that the groundskeepers needed to use to maintain the Honey Hills Center's property. Jacob kept his hand in Bess's hand and every so often he would ask her a question about a piece of equipment he didn't recognize. From all of her walks around the grounds, Bess was able to answer every question Jacob had. For a moment, she was reminded of the days when she would take Samantha to the zoo. She was reminded of how Samantha would hold her hand, point at things, and ask her questions about animals she didn't know. As she did with Samantha, Bess patiently answered every question that Jacob asked. In a matter of minutes, they had examined everything that was kept in the barn. When they walked back out the door, Jacob looked up at Bess and smiled.

"Now that we've solved this mystery... how would you like to help me solve another one?" Bess asked, carefully closing the barn door.

Jacob nodded his head and waited patiently for Bess to reveal the details of another mystery.

"This is a mystery about a disappearing boy," Bess began, carefully latching the barn door shut. "Once there was a boy that a group of children loved. A boy that even the teachers loved. Then one morning, when no one was looking, the boy simply vanished without a trace. Well, of course his friends and his teachers were quite concerned. They looked everywhere…but no one could find the boy who disappeared. Now all of his friends and teachers are quite sad…because no one knows what happened to him. It's a mystery."

Jacob smiled.

"I think…you're talking about me," Jacob said with a bashful grin.

"Am I?" Bess asked, and both her eyebrows went up. "Did you make someone sad this morning, Jacob? Did you disappear?"

"I guess," Jacob answered and he shrugged his shoulders. "I didn't mean to make anyone sad. I just wanted to go see the farm animals."

"I think you've solved another mystery, Jacob," Bess smiled and she gently took Jacob's hand. "Let's go back and solve this mystery for your friends, too. They will be most happy to see you again."

Together they walked back up the road towards the main building of the Honey Hills Center. As they walked, Bess noticed the lush green grass, the bright green leaves, and the occasional bird that sweetly sang when they moved by an arcing branch of a nearby tree. Yet, despite all the beauty that surrounded her, there was something else that made Bess smile. She looked down at the small boy holding her hand. Without knowing it, Jacob had just solved one more mystery for Bess. What made a walk on such a beautiful spring morning even better? Having a hand to hold.

CARDS AND CROISSANTS

"Croissants," Rose Grumbine grinned from her seat. She scooped up a deck of cards, began to shuffle them, and smiled. Her red lips parted, revealing bright white teeth that matched the curls and swirls of her hair. Rose had her hair washed once a week at the Honey Hills Center's beauty parlor. It was a luxury that not many of the ladies at the Honey Hills could afford. Having owned a chain of flower shops, Rose was wealthy enough to afford such pampering. "Do any of you know how much I look forward to breakfast because of those croissants our new chef keeps making?"

"I never had one before this month," Flo Morganstern jumped in. She looked around at her friends and shrugged her shoulders. "It's true. Ever since I was a girl I had cereal and toast for breakfast. Never had a croissant. Now, thanks to that new chef, I can't imagine starting my day without one. After a few weeks that new chef has me hooked on croissants. What is his name again?"

"His name is Tony," Alma jumped in. "I heard that Tony graduated from Grantham College."

"We should write Grantham a big thank you note," Flo laughed.

"What happened to the last cook?" Bess asked.

"Same thing that happened to the one before that," Rose replied. "You see, Bess, they all come here right out of college. They all stay here for a year or two. They get some experience. Then they start to get better job offers with more money. That's when they leave. It's gotten to the point where I don't even know their names anymore. Give this new one some time, he'll be baking pastries at a high end restaurant sooner or later. They want the money and they're not gonna find that working at a retirement home."

So it was at the Honey Hills Center, Bess thought. People came and people went. For every resident who passed on, another took their place. Happily, Bess thought, the chefs left for all together different reasons than the residents.

"This one is better than the last chef," Bess observed. She drew in her breath. "I'm not just talking about the croissants. The soups, the desserts, the dinners, everything he makes just tastes wonderful. In fact, judging by the buzz around here, I'd be willing to bet this chef is better than most of the chefs you've ever had at the Honey Hills Center. Am I right, ladies?"

Flo and Alma turned to look at Rose, who had been there longer than anyone at the table.

"By far the best," Rose nodded and she bit her bottom lip to reflect on her judgment. She was quiet for a few seconds then slowly nodded her head. "I've never tasted food like this since coming here."

Bess leaned back in her chair, pulled up her cards to her face and grew silent on the topic of Tony the chef.

"What's the matter, Bess?" Rose asked. "Don't you like his cooking?"

"Yes," Bess mumbled from behind her cards. "Everything he makes tastes good. I'm just wondering if…he's just too good to be working here."

"Oh no," Flo mumbled.

"What?" Alma asked, lowering her cards.

"I know that look," Flo announced. Her eyes shifted to Bess and she pointed across the table at her.

"Don't tell me you think it's strange that we have a good cook?"

"He's talented," Bess explained, lowering her cards and tapping them on the table. "We all know how well he cooks. I mean...why would someone that talented settle for working in a retirement home? It just seems rather odd to me...that's all."

"Bess Bullock!" Flo snapped and her voice grew sharper and louder. "Don't you go poking around the chef, Bess! We're lucky to have him. He makes good food...so just leave it at that!"

"Flo," Alma said with a smile. "Why would you say that? Do you think Bess is really going to drive him away?"

"I know Bess," Flo replied, sitting up to the table and resting her elbows on it. "She's gonna say or do something to solve a mystery about this young man...then he's gonna pack up and leave. Now I don't know about the rest of you...but I like having my croissant in the morning for breakfast. I like looking forward to eating tasty foods for a change. I just don't want Bess to meddle in a good thing...that's all."

"You worry too much, Flo," Bess quietly stated.

Bess sat up to the table and focused on the cards in her hand. While she waited for the first cards to be played, Bess thought about Chef Tony. How would she find a way to meet him? How would she investigate her suspicions?

INTO THE KITCHEN

Bess sat quietly at her table after dinner and smiled blankly at the empty plate in front of her. For this evening's meal, Chef Tony had managed to prepare a very tender chicken breast that he marinated in a sweet sauce she didn't recognize but clearly loved. Her eyes glided around the room, watching Willie Nagel clear the tables. Willie's eyes glanced over at Bess and she thought that she was making him nervous with her presence. He wasn't even attempting to eat any left over food and was very quick at taking the dishes into the kitchen. Finally, Bess stood up and walked over to Willie.

"Excuse me, Willie," Bess said with a smile. "I just had the best dinner I've eaten in a long time. Do you think you could walk me into the kitchen so I could thank Chef Tony?"

"Of course…but he's very busy," Willie replied.

Together they walked back to the kitchen, with Willie carrying a tray of dirty dishes. When they reached the kitchen, Willie put the tray down and reached into a basket of dinner rolls that had not been eaten. He looked at Bess, held the dinner roll up between them and smiled.

"This didn't come off of anyone's plate," Willie announced.

"Very good, Willie," Bess replied with a tone of voice she once used as a mother.

Bess followed Willie back through the kitchen. She walked by some metal tables and could smell some food that was still lingering in the air. She spotted a young man, dressed in white pants and a white top with a white apron tied around his waist. His hair was short, one shade lighter than brown. His face was red and he appeared to be placing a metal bowl back on a shelf. When he turned, it was hard not to notice his bright blue eyes fixed above his red cheeks. They were light blue like the kind of ocean someone would spot from a Caribbean island. While she'd never been to such a place, Bess had seen pictures and found the water just as bright and blue.

"Hey, Tony," Willie spoke up. "I got someone here who wants to meet you."

Bess watched Chef Tony wipe his hands with a towel and step over to her.

"Hello. Chef Tony?" Bess said. "I doubt you'll remember me. You gave me a box of croissants not too long ago. My name is Mrs. Bullock."

"I remember," Chef Tony replied. He folded his arms, gave a measured smile, and walked over to where Bess and Willie were standing. "You said the croissants were for Willie. Do you want more croissants? I'm afraid I won't have any until tomorrow morning."

"No, no, I'm not here for croissants," Bess quickly answered and she waved her hand in the air. "I wanted to thank you for dinner tonight. Well...I should really thank you for everything you've been making around here. The croissants, the soups, the deserts, everything has just been wonderful."

"Well I'm glad you are enjoying my food," Chef Tony replied.

"I know quite a few residents have said the same thing," Bess continued. "You've made such an impact with the people here. Your gift of cooking has just...taken us out of our routine days and given us something wonderful to look forward to. Thank you again."

Chef Tony simply nodded at the compliment but instead of smiling, he simply folded his arms and kept an empty expression on his face. Strangely, Bess thought, he didn't have too much to say in return. Bess could sense that he appreciated the kind words. Yet, there was something in his face. Something in how he looked and how he dropped his eyes to the floor during a pause in their conversation.

"How did you find our little retirement home?" Bess asked.

"Just lucky I guess," Chef Tony explained, and he pulled out a damp towel and nervously wiped his hands with it. His hands were perfectly clean, Bess thought, and yet he was wiping them on the towel like they were covered in dirt.

"Do you have any plans to leave?" Bess pressed. "You see, a lot of our chefs use the Honey Hills Center as a stepping stone to bigger and better things."

"I have no plans to leave," Tony simply answered.

"But you're truly quite talented," Bess said. "We've had our share of chefs come and go over the years. I've been here about a year, but I can hear what the other ladies are saying. Your food is by far...the best. Any of the ladies here at Honey Hills will testify to that. Why would you settle for working here?"

"I have my reasons," Chef Tony mumbled and he grabbed a cutting board and began to wipe it off.

Bess could sense the wall he had built with his words. She didn't want to press him too much for fear of putting him on the defensive. His decision was a private one and for now she had to respect that. She watched his eyes move away from her and linger to the side of the kitchen where the sink was filled with dirty pots, pans and baking sheets. She also spotted a mound of dirty dishes piled on a counter next to the sink.

"Well," Bess said, with a nod, "I can see you have a lot of work to do. I'll leave you and Willie to clean up."

Chef Tony offered one measured smile before he turned and resumed wiping down his counter and stacking a few more bowls in the sink.

Bess made her way out of the kitchen to the sound of clanging pots and running water.

For as warm and inviting as his food had been, Bess found Chef Tony to be just the opposite. He seemed a bit distant to her. He also seemed a bit elusive in answering her questions. She remembered how he vigorously wiped his hands after she inquired about his employment at Honey Hills. She also recalled how his cheeks grew flushed when she pressed him on his timetable to leave.

Bess paused and looked back at Willie and Chef Tony working together in the kitchen. She listened to their conversation and comments. There seemed to be an air of ease between the two men. It was the kind of easy conversation Bess had hoped to have with Chef Tony.

Perhaps, she thought, Willie would be the key to getting Chef Tony to open up.

"You know, Tony," Bess began, stepping back into the kitchen. "Willie here has always had an interest in cooking. He's told me more than once about the things he makes and the articles he's read about cooking."

"I have?" Willie asked.

Bess winked at Willie.

"Oh yes," Willie nodded, seeming to understand Bess's plan.

"Now of course he is a volunteer here at Honey Hills," Bess stated. "Could you use him as a volunteer apprentice here in your kitchen? Someone to assist and learn from you?"

"Is this true, Willie?" Tony asked. "Do you like to cook?"

Willie glanced over at Bess and she could tell he was tongue tied. Bess nodded once to Willie who turned to Chef Tony and forced a smile.

"I'm a bachelor," Willie quickly explained. "I cook all the time."

"Well, I'm not sure..." Tony began and then his voice drifted into silence.

"I can tell you could use an assistant when I look at this place," Bess said, turning around and gesturing at the mounds of dishes with her hands. "I can only imagine how much easier it would be to clean up this mess with an assistant. Now I know Willie volunteers in the dining room, but he could shift his efforts into the kitchen. I'm sure Willie would be of great service with food prep and clean up. I'm quite certain he would be an asset in your kitchen, too."

Chef Tony nodded at the words. He took a step back, folded his arms, looked Willie up and down.

"I know you work hard. You do a fine job of cleaning up the dining room, Willie," Chef Tony began. "Would you be willing to come in earlier and help me with preparing three meals a day? It's a big responsibility and there are a lot of people counting on good meals."

"I'll work hard," Willie quickly nodded.

"Good," Chef Tony said and his face melted into the most pleasant smile Bess could ever have imagined. "I'll make sure you get three good meals a day for your work. If you'd like, you can eat with me, Willie. It'll be nice having someone to eat with for a change."

"No more table scraps," Bess whispered into Willie's ear.

"Thank you," Willie grinned to Tony. "What time should I be here tomorrow?"

"Six in the morning," Tony quickly answered. "You know how early breakfast gets served around here. So I'll see you back here at six o'clock?"

"I'll be here," Willie grinned.

"Let me show you a few things before you leave," Chef Tony said and he took Willie by the arm and led him to a giant mixer in the far corner of the kitchen.

Bess quietly showed herself out of the kitchen. She paused and looked back to see Willie and Chef Tony speak by the stove. While it was the first time she'd ever wandered into the kitchen, it was also the happiest she'd ever felt leaving the dining room.

THE PUZZLE OF DUTCH

It was a Tuesday morning, the best morning of the week for Bess Bullock. It was the morning that she began by sitting around a table with her friends, dealing cards, sharing thoughts and enjoying the game of bridge. It was easy to take such mornings for granted, but for six days a week Bess found very little company that matched her friends. Living in the Honey Hills Center meant there were many days of polite smiles to fellow residents in the halls, occasional naps in an easy chair, and the infrequent visits from her daughter, Samantha. Yet, with all of these people filling her days, the conversations she enjoyed most were the ones spent with friends.

"There's a new lady in my wing from India," Flo Morgenstern stated while she shuffled cards for another round of Bridge. "I've never known anyone from India before. She is very sweet to talk to. She owns some very beautiful clothes. Very polite at dinner, too."

"Speaking of dinner," Alma began. "Wasn't that Chocolate Mousse simply divine? I think I'm beginning to enjoy Chef Tony's deserts more than his dinners."

"I agree," Rose laughed. "Anything with chocolate makes me happy."

"Desserts aren't for me," Flo replied. "I like his dinners much more. Take yesterday's dinner for example. I thought the pork he served last night was wonderful. I've loved pork since I was a girl. The way it was served with rice and that sauce...I think it was some kind of apple sauce he made. Oh…that was more delicious than any desert he could make for me."

While Rose Grumbine began to respond to Flo's words, Bess found her eyes drifting away from the conversation. Her eyes moved to the open door to the book room, where she saw a figure quickly walking up the hall. It was a man with thick white hair and a large round stomach that easily distracted from his short legs, stocky arms and slight neck. His lips were mashed together and he appeared slightly hunched over his feet while he used a cane to walk. Bess recognized the figure as being Bill "Dutch" Howard.

Dutch wasn't someone Bess spoke to very often. There was something about him that made him a bit unapproachable to Bess. It started with the expression on his face, which was always serious no matter if he was walking the halls or eating in the dining room. Whenever he walked by Bess in the hallway, his eyes would narrow and his smile looked measured, almost polite. The only thing Bess was sure of about Dutch was the well polished silver eagle that sat proudly on top of his walking cane. The eagle's wings were drawn in and its chest puffed out much like Dutch's, Bess thought. Bess leaned back in her seat and took a deep breath when she saw Dutch in the doorway. It appeared he was staring at her and no one else.

"Ladies," Dutch growled from the doorway. He took a few steps into the room and stopped in front of their table, the eagle on his cane flashing in the light. Dutch looked around at Bess, Rose, Flo and Alma. His bright red face made his white hair look even brighter. He curled his fingers and leaned forward so his knuckles were on the table. His large round stomach rested on the table and came dangerously close to their cards.

"Is there something you need?" Flo asked.

"Puzzle club," Dutch grumbled and his eyes narrowed. "Do you ladies even know we have a puzzle club here at the Honey Hills Center?"

"I've seen signs advertising the club," Flo nodded. "Puzzles are too boring for me…so I've never attended a meeting."

"Well," Dutch began. "I'm the president of the puzzle club. Now ladies, I have an important matter to discuss with Mrs. Bullock about my club. May I speak with you in the hallway, Mrs. Bullock?"

"Of course, Dutch," Bess smiled. She quietly stood up and led Dutch out of the room.

"Can you take a walk with me, Mrs. Bullock?" Dutch asked, jabbing his cane forward.

"Of course," Bess replied, following Dutch down the hall. "Where are we going?"

"Nowhere," Dutch said. "Walking helps me think a little better."

"So what can I help you with, Dutch?" Bess asked.

"We have a puzzle thief in our midst," Dutch replied.

"Excuse me?" Bess said. She felt her stomach jump and her mouth curled up at the corners. A mystery had quite unexpectedly presented itself. Judging by the butterflies in her stomach, Bess could sense her instincts were clearly happy with the development.

"I need you to catch a puzzle thief," Dutch stated with the kind of seriousness that seemed to undercut the lighthearted nature of his statement. Bess was now fully engaged by the mystery Dutch was about to present. Dutch used his cane with great precision, moving faster and faster down the hall. Bess quickened her pace to keep up with him, anxious to learn more details about his request.

"Can you tell me more?" Bess asked, thinking she misheard Dutch.

"There's a puzzle thief in my puzzle club," Dutch continued. "I need you to catch the thief."

"I see," Bess said. "So what can you tell me about this…puzzle thief?"

DUTCH'S CLUB

"About a year ago, I started a Flag Committee," Dutch began. "The group is comprised of a few of us war vets who raise and lower the flag every day here at the Honey Hills Center. A couple of us from this group also share a mutual interest in jigsaw puzzles. We were the first ones to form the Puzzle Club. In the last year we've taken on some new members. Some are friends we know...so we're a tight group. Anyway, as president of the club it's my responsibility to purchase the puzzles that our group undertakes."

Dutch sniffed and stopped at a window. He leaned on his cane and glanced out at fields of tall green corn swaying in a breeze. His eyes narrowed while he stared at the scene.

"Now I like to challenge my group," Dutch said with some pride in his voice. "So I'll take a bus into town and try to shop for the hardest puzzles I can find. Puzzles with pieces that can total in the thousands. Puzzles that have unique curves or patterns. No matter what type of puzzle I can find...my group always seems to wrap it up in about a month. We only meet for an hour a day, but during the course of the month the puzzle really pushes our skills and forces us to focus."

"Two months ago," Dutch continued, "we completed a puzzle of the Taj Mahal. Beautiful picture of the structure. Vivid colors. Just wonderful to see...but we had one problem."

"What was that?" Bess asked.

"A missing puzzle piece," Dutch mumbled. He turned away from the window and the corn field and focused on Bess.

"I cannot tell you how frustrating it is to work on a puzzle and not be able to see it to completion," Dutch grunted. He tapped his cane on the floor once and shook his head. "My group was very disappointed, as was I."

"Perhaps it was lost," Bess suggested.

"Not likely," Dutch answered. "I cracked open the box right after I bought it. I counted each piece to insure that they were all present. There were no missing pieces when I checked that puzzle."

"I see," Bess said, her eyes shifting to the floor. "Perhaps it got lost during the assembling. I mean, those puzzle pieces can be very tiny, Dutch."

"Yes," Dutch nodded. "I thought as much, too. The next month I went shopping again and I bought a gorgeous puzzle of the Grand Canyon. There were many shades of red, pink, orange and lavender that made this puzzle a challenge to work on. After a few meetings we managed to assemble it…but once again there was a piece missing."

"Really?" Bess said with a slow nod. She could feel her eyebrows lower, which is what usually happened when she was focused on something. At the moment, Dutch was what she was focused on. "So you were missing a piece. Did you count the pieces for that puzzle too?"

"Yes," Dutch answered. "I cut open the box the night before and checked every piece myself. I checked it twice, actually. All the pieces were there, Mrs. Bullock. My wife watched me count them. Yet, once again a piece went missing. It's been quite frustrating for myself and my club, Mrs. Bullock."

"I can imagine," Bess nodded in agreement.

"Now there are more than a few members who are pretty upset about this. In fact, some members have talked about quitting the puzzle club," Dutch said. He looked down at his shoes and tapped the tip of his shoe with his cane. "I've heard them grumble about it and I know some of them are quite angry with me."

"You?" Bess asked. "Why would they suspect you?"

"They seem to think I may be culpable for the theft," Dutch explained. "I told them I wasn't…and that's when a small argument broke out at our last meeting. The only solution we came up with was to have you watch me count the pieces whenever I bought a puzzle."

"Me?" Bess asked.

"I thought you could come to my room and witness me count the puzzle pieces for our latest puzzle," Dutch suggested. He looked at her and for the first time Bess noticed that his eyes did not narrow in that same look of disdain he usually gave her or any other woman at the Honey Hills Center.

"Why would they ask for me?" Bess asked.

"You have a reputation here at Honey Hills," Dutch explained. "A good many members of my group asked for you by name to help in this matter. They trust you, Mrs. Bullock. Could you come by my room this afternoon? How does four o'clock sound?"

"I think that would be fine," Bess answered.

"If I'm not there my wife will be there," Dutch answered. He extended his hand to Bess.

When she slipped her hand into his he gave it a firm grip and a measured shake. "I'll see you this afternoon, Mrs. Bullock. Thank you for your help in this matter."

Bess stayed by the window and watched Dutch slowly hobble down the hallway with his cane. She often regarded Dutch as being one of the toughest men at Honey Hills. She knew of his military service and his gruff way of speaking to others. She also knew he took great pride in the brass eagle that sat on top of his cane. He was military through and through and proud of it. Now, this man that she had assumed was so tough, needed her help because of a small puzzle piece. Bess couldn't help but smile at the irony.

PUTTING THE PIECES TOGETHER

Dutch's room was a long hike from where Bess lived in the Honey Hills Center. He was located in an older wing at the opposite end of the building. Bess was reminded of this when she moved from the plush blue green rug in her hallway to the dull tan and brown tiled floor of the older wing. With her shoes clapping on the linoleum tiles, Bess easily found Dutch's room. The door to the room was opened wide. She looked inside where she found a small woman seated on a rocking chair watching television. Her large round glasses glowed from the light of the television. When she saw Bess standing in the doorway, the woman turned off her television and stood up to greet Bess.

"Mrs. Bullock?" she asked.

"Yes," Bess smiled, stepping into the room. "Are you Dutch's wife?"

"I am," the woman smiled. "My name is Nell Howard. We've actually exchanged greetings in the hallway a few times. I've also seen you walking out on the grounds some mornings. I too enjoy a good walk to start the day."

"I thought your face looked familiar," Bess replied, trying to put Nell at ease. "I wasn't sure of your name…but I do remember seeing your face."

"So you're going to help my husband?" Nell asked, placing her TV remote down by her chair.

"I will try," Bess answered. She looked around at the spacious room and then she turned to the bathroom where she saw the door was open and the lights off. "Where is Dutch?"

"Oh," Nell sighed and she waved her hands in the air. "There's not a whole lotta ground that grows under Dutch's feet. In the morning, he gets up early and goes off with his Flag Committee to raise the flag up the flag pole by the entrance to the Honey Hills Center parking lot. After that, sometimes he and his buddies go for a cup of coffee down at the dining room."

"I see," Bess nodded, glancing over at the time on the clock.

"Oh, don't worry," Nell smiled. "He'll be here soon. A little while later he'll duck out again to meet with his Puzzle Club. In the evening he likes to go into town to the local VFW to chat with some other vets. I don't care for the bad language...so I choose not to go along."

"I see," Bess nodded.

"Yes," Nell mumbled. She settled down in her chair and looked at Bess. "Were you ever married, Mrs. Bullock?"

"I was," Bess answered.

"Did you have an idea of how you would spend your final years with your spouse?" Nell asked.

"My husband died a few years ago," Bess answered. She looked down and glanced at the gold ring on her one finger. "I never had the luxury to entertain the kind of thoughts you're talking about."

"I'm sorry," Nell replied. She laced her fingers together and rested her hands on her lap. "I thought Dutch and I would enjoy our time here together. I know Dutch has been enjoying his many activities...but I thought we'd spend more time together when we moved here. Some days...I feel more like a widow than a wife."

When she ended her comment, Bess noticed how Nell's eyes dropped down to her hands. Her fingers were laced around her hands with a tight grip. Watching her face, and her hands, something in Bess felt that Nell's words were the tip of the iceberg. That somewhere deep down, she harbored stronger feelings about Dutch and his activities. Feelings she probably didn't share with anyone.

"Good morning, Mrs. Bullock!" a man's voice boomed from the doorway.

The voice caused Bess to turn around to find Dutch walking into the room. Without breaking stride, Dutch dropped his keys into a glass tray, kissed Nell, and smiled at Bess.

"Was it a good morning for a flag raising?" Nell asked.

"Blue sky and sunshine," Dutch replied with a quick wink. "It doesn't get any better."

Nell offered a tired smile at the words, then turned the television back on and folded her arms. It struck Bess that the comment seemed like part of their morning routine. The casual way the words were spoken. The disinterested way that Nell reacted to the answer. It was almost like she heard the answer a thousand times before and knew what Dutch would say before he spoke.

"Well, let's get right to it," Dutch announced and he grabbed a box from a shelf and walked over to a small table in the corner of the room. He sat down, placed his cane next to his chair and handed the box to Bess.

"You can see it hasn't been opened?" Dutch asked.

"Yes," Bess nodded, admiring the rich colors that made up the picture of the canyon. She then checked the sides of the box and could see it was still sealed.

Dutch snatched the box away from Bess, tore open the sides, and dumped the pieces out on the table.

"Now you stay here," Dutch stated, wagging his finger at Bess. "You listen to me count, Mrs. Bullock. You watch to make sure I don't miss any pieces. This might take a little while so get yourself comfy. You want a drink or anything? Nell can get you something to drink if you'd like one."

"No thank you," Bess said, and she raised her hand towards Nell. "I'm not thirsty. Why don't you begin to count, Dutch."

In the moments that followed, the only sound Bess heard was the gravely voice of Dutch counting each puzzle piece. She kept her eyes on the table and watched his large thick fingers paw at one puzzle piece after another, pulling them to the center of the table Bess kept her eyes focused on Dutch and part of her felt like she was a mother again, helping her daughter master the art of counting. Every so often, Bess would let her eyes drift off the table. Her eyes would settle on Nell, who sat with her eyes directed to the floor, despite the fact that the television was on. Every so often, Bess would see Nell's hand dip into a side pocket to her chair and reappear again. Bess found her eyes more interested in watching Nell than Dutch.

"Do you have any thoughts on this matter, Mrs. Howard?" Bess finally spoke up.

"Me?" Nell asked. "Thoughts on what?"

"Your husband is being accused of lying to the other members of his puzzle club," Bess explained. "It is a shame to see a man's good name become soiled by something as silly as a few missing puzzle pieces. I'd be interested to know your thoughts on this matter."

Nell shifted in her seat, like she was uncomfortable in her chair for the first time since Bess entered the room. Nell's hand continued to dangle by a small pouch that was built into the arm rest of her chair. Her fingers nervously fiddled in the pocket. Bess stepped closer to Nell, whose eyes were now turned out the window.

"Certainly you have an opinion," Bess stated and she gave her voice a shaper tone. "I'm afraid Dutch may not be thought of very well by the other people in his Puzzle Club. Some are questioning his honesty. I would think you might have something to say about the accusations."

The words caused Nell to dip her hand deep into the side pocket of her chair. While Dutch continued to count his puzzle pieces, Bess watched as Nell stared at the floor and nervously fiddled with something in the pocket of her chair.

"Is your husband a liar?" Bess asked.

She watched as Nell's hand emerged from the side pocket of her chair. In her hand, Bess expected to see a tissue or even a pen. Instead, Nell's hand emerged with two stray puzzle pieces. Nell didn't say anything. She remained seated, staring at the puzzle pieces in her hand. Bess stood over her and then turned her eyes to Dutch who was still counting puzzle pieces at the table. Finally, Dutch met Bess's gaze and stepped away from the table. He walked over and looked at what was in Nell's hand. He reached down, took the pieces out of her hand and closely examined each one. He looked at her and held out his hand with the pieces in it.

"Nell!" he snapped, his face growing a darker shade of red. "It was you? You were the one who stole these pieces from our last puzzle? What in blazes did you do that for?"

"Wait, Dutch," Bess stated in a tone of voice that was as loud as she could speak. "I think there is a reason for this...isn't there Nell."

"What are you talking about?" Dutch grunted. He turned to Bess, his eyes narrowed, and he held out the pieces in his hand. "She made me look like a fool to my friends."

"Perhaps," Bess nodded. She looked at Nell and rested her hand on Nell's shoulder. "I suspect there is another reason...isn't there Nell. You know, Nell and I had a chance to chat before you came, Dutch. She told me about your schedule...with the flag committee, your trips to the local VFW and of course your Puzzle Club. With so many responsibilities it doesn't seem to give you much time to spend with your wife...does it?"

Dutch's eyes narrowed and he mumbled something under his breath. He reached down to Nell's hand and helped her out of her chair. He stood in front of her, toe to toe, and looked down at her.

"You're never around," Nell finally said with a whisper.

"I didn't know it bothered you," Dutch replied, and he reached down and took her small hand in his much larger one. He rubbed her wedding ring with his thumb and for a brief moment, Bess felt like she was invisible to both of them. "Of course I can make time for us. I can stop going to the VFW so we could have our evenings together."

"And about that flag committee," Nell stated. "I don't mind you going out and raising the flag, Dutch. I think that's important. I just wish you and your fellas wouldn't spend so much time together having coffee afterwards. I'd like to wake up and find you here. Waking up to an empty room...well I feel like a widow."

"That will change," Dutch smiled. "I promise."

Bess lowered her head and quietly stepped out of the room. In one swift motion, her instincts had led her eyes to Nell and her fingers that were nervously tapping the bag next to her chair. She hoped that Dutch would follow through on his promise. She knew what it felt like to be a widow. She hoped Nell wouldn't have to feel that way again.

CHECKING IN WITH WILLIE

A week had gone by and Bess was curious about Willie. She hadn't seen him all that much around the Honey Hills Center and she hoped everything was going well for him and Chef Tony. One afternoon she finished off a ham and cheese sandwich for lunch and then lingered in the dining room. She waited and watched Willie slip out of the kitchen door and begin to clean up the plates. She sipped her coffee and observed him carry the dirty dishes into the kitchen for a few minutes. Finally, she stood up and peeked in through the door to the kitchen. She was able to see Willie hard at work washing dishes in the sink. Chef Tony was at a long table preparing food for dinner. Both men were calling out to each other, discussing a baseball game they had watched the night before. From the sound of it, Bess guessed they liked the same team which gave her some relief knowing they had at least one thing to talk about.

"Chef Tony," Bess said, stepping into the kitchen. She walked over to the table where Chef Tony was working. She folded her hands in front of her waist and stood by for a few seconds while she watched Chef Tony chop carrots into small pieces with a large knife.

"Is there something I can help you with, Mrs. Bullock?" Chef Tony asked, waving his knife in the air between chops.

"I was just checking in on Willie. How is he working out for you?" Bess asked.

"Willie is doing a good job," Chef Tony replied, grabbing another carrot and cutting it into small pieces. "He's helping me with food prep and cleaning up in the kitchen after meals. Things are running much smoother with Willie around. I may start training him to help me prepare the actual meals, soon. He has a real interest in what I'm doing."

"Willie is a good man," Bess replied. "He has a keen interest in learning lots of things. I've seen him with the nurses here at Honey Hills. They've instructed him on helping them with some things and he's been very quick to pick it up."

"I can see that here, too," Chef Tony said. "He does learn things quickly."

"Good," Bess nodded. She looked down at the chopping block and tapped her hand on it.

"What's for dinner tonight?"

"We're going to have a soufflé for desert this evening," Chef Tony replied. "As soon as I'm done cutting the carrots for my soup, I have a lot of eggs to crack for my soufflé so I really do have a good amount of work to do."

"You sound very busy," Bess observed and when she finished her sentence she found herself simply staring at Chef Tony while he began to chop another carrot.

"Was there something else?" Chef Tony asked, raising his knife in the air before waiting for Bess to answer his question.

"Yes," Bess said, and she grabbed hold of a small chopped carrot and pulled it off the cutting board. "Why *are* you working here?"

Chef Tony laid his knife down on the table and turned his head to one side.

"It's my job," he replied. "Where else would you want me to be, Mrs. Bullock?"

"It is well known around the hallways that you're the best chef we've ever had at the Honey Hills Center," Bess began. "From your meals right down to your croissants, your skills as a chef are far above anyone we've ever had here. This then begs the question of why you are here. Are you here because this was the only job you could find? I understand you graduated from Grantham College, which has a fine reputation for being one of the best culinary schools in the state. Graduating from their culinary program must have been quite an accomplishment. With how well you cook, and where you graduated from, I would guess you had your choice of places to work. Maybe some fancy hotels. Maybe some elegant restaurants that charge twenty dollars for a glass of wine and a lot more for a dinner. I doubt a retirement home was your only option. So that takes me back to my first question…why are you working here?"

Chef Tony looked at Bess. He lowered his knife down on the cutting board. He glanced over his shoulder at Willie, who was elbow deep in washing dishes and rinsing. Chef Tony took a deep breath and looked back to Bess. She could tell he was uncertain of what to do. She offered him her most comforting smile.

"Please," she softly said. "Please tell me why."

TONY THE CHEF'S STORY

"When I was in high school, I remember why grandma was moved to the Honey Hills Center. It was right after my grandpa died. Grandma Cordaro lived by herself in a row home for many years. Then my mom decided that it wasn't safe for her to live there anymore. When Grandma Cordaro moved here my mom told me that grandma was very angry. She didn't like being taken away from her home. She even told my mom that she wished someone would shoot her," Chef Tony recalled.

"It can be a difficult transition," Bess nodded. "Everyone is different. Some of us find the move easier than others."

"Well after a few weeks," Chef Tony continued, "my grandma began to like the place. I remember how my mother and I would visit her every Sunday. I'd listen to my mother's conversations with grandma and I remember thinking that my grandma had started to become happy with her new home. After living in the isolation of a row home in the city, Grandma Cordaro was enjoying being around people her own age. She would eat at a table with other women and when they spoke, I think she discovered they had a lot in common. She started to go to Bingo. I went with her one time and noticed how much she liked laughing with the other ladies. She even started to attend craft classes and rediscovered how much she loved to paint. She was making friends. She was around people and I think she discovered how much she had been missing in her life when she was in that row home."

"There are a lot of nice people here," Bess agreed.

"She spent six years here at the Honey Hills Center," Chef Tony stated. He picked up a knife and carefully wiped it clean. "When she died, she fell asleep and quietly passed away. Our family only had positive things to say about the Honey Hills Center and the nurses who cared for Grandma Cordaro. I think…they kinda became her family during her stay here."

Chef Tony paused and looked down at his cutting board. He carefully placed the knife down on his board.

"The only negative part of my grandma's experience came after her death," Chef Tony sighed. "You see, there was something that was taken from her when she died. It was a ring that she never took off. As long as I can remember my Grandma, I can remember this big sparkly diamond ring that she wore. I remember how it flashed in the sunlight, like she was wearing a sparkle on her hand. She wore it day and night and never took it off. The day Grandma Cordaro died, my mother and her two sisters were the first to notice it was gone. The ring contained a rather large diamond and it once belonged to her mother. Great-Grandma Cordaro was quite rich, or so I've been told. If I close my eyes, I can still see grandma sitting in her chair, nervously turning the ring with her fingers while she listened to me talk about things. When she died, I think we were all stunned to learn that the ring Grandma Cordaro never took off…was suddenly gone."

"Oh my," Bess said. She stepped closer to Chef Tony and looked him in the eye. "Do you think it was stolen?"

"We don't know," Chef Tony answered. "My mother and her sisters talked to the nurses, and the cleaning ladies, and the director of the Honey Hills Center. They hung around here for weeks asking lots of questions, but the ring was never recovered. While my mother and sisters quietly accepted this fact, I still feel that the ring is somewhere around here at the Honey Hills Center. When I saw the job of cooking for the Honey Hills Center was posted at my college, I quickly pursued it. Some of my classmates were fielding more lucrative offers and they couldn't believe I was going to settle for working here. They didn't understand. I chose to come here on the chance that one day…I'll find my grandmother's ring and return it to our family."

"A ring?" Bess said and she shook her head in disbelief. "A cook as skilled and talented as you…that's why you're here…to find a ring?"

"I hope that solves your mystery, Mrs. Bullock. Now I must get back to work," Chef Tony said. He lowered his eyes, grabbed a tomato, and began slicing it with his knife.

Bess quietly turned and walked out of the kitchen. Indeed, Chef Tony's words had solved one mystery for Bess. However, just as his words had created resolution for one matter, they had opened up another mystery. What had happened to the ring of Grandma Cordaro?

GRANDMA CORDARO'S FOOTSTEPS

From her conversation with Chef Tony, Bess was quick to conclude that she'd never met Grandma Cordaro. It sounded as though Grandma Cordaro had lived at the Honey Hills Center before Bess had arrived. If there was one truth about a retirement home, Bess thought, it was that the faces of its residents never stayed the same for very long. Established residents died and new residents were always moving in to replace them. Most of the residents Bess was acquainted with were relatively new to the Honey Hills Center. Bess got the impression that Grandma Cordaro was at Honey Hills years ago. To the best of her knowledge, Bess knew that none of her bridge club friends had been at Honey Hills that long. In fact, there was only one person Bess could think of who may have been at the Honey Hills Center longer than anyone.

Ruth Moore was going on one hundred and one years old. Bess first met Ruth at a centennial birthday party thrown in her honor last year. Since then Bess had made a point to visit Ruth Moore now and then. She found Ruth's stories fascinating to listen to and always enjoyed her company. After all, Bess reasoned, a woman who lived for one hundred years wouldn't have boring stories to tell. Hopefully her memory was sharp enough to remember Grandma Cordaro, Bess hoped.

"Ruth," Bess called out with a gentle wrap on the door. "Ruth…it's me…Bess."

"Come in," a delicate voice answered.

Bess opened the door to find Ruth Moore, sitting in her wheelchair, a magnifying glass in one hand and a book on her lap.   Ruth was an avid reader and Bess remembered hearing Ruth say that she tried to read one book a week, even at the age of one hundred.

"Hello, Bess," Ruth said, her small mouth turning up at the corners.   She lowered her magnifying glass onto the open book.

"Good morning, Ruth," Bess said, sitting down in an empty chair beside Ruth.   She pointed to Ruth's lap. "And what book are you reading this morning."

"Louisa May Alcott," Ruth quickly answered.   Her blues eyes appeared to light up at the fact that she was being engaged in conversation. "I found a copy of *Little Women* in the library and I had to borrow it."

"I never read it," Bess admitted.

"Oh, Bess, you have to," Ruth quickly advised. "The story is just so touching. You know I was the youngest of three sisters, so I could relate to the story's main character, Jo."

"I had a brother," Bess nodded. "He was younger than me.   There's a lot of responsibility to being a big sister. I was always the one helping my mother and my father around the house. My little brother was too busy with other things to help with the chores."

"There are indeed some things about family we just never forget," Ruth said, and she closed her book with a magnifying glass marking her page.

"Yes," Bess nodded.   "How long have lived in Honey Hills, Ruth?"

"Ten years," Ruth sighed, nervously tapping the white curls that rode above her ears with her fingers. "When I first arrived at Honey Hills I was driving my own car, taking my friends to restaurants once a week. I even proctored a college class on computers. Moving here for me...it was just geography, Bess. It didn't change who I was or what I did. My body got old but I refused to let my mind age with it."

Bess nodded at the words and felt a kind of kinship with Ruth. Even though she had moved to a retirement home, Bess also found that the move hadn't changed her powers of observation or her investigative instincts. The thought brought her back to her original reason for visiting Ruth Moore.

"I need to test your memory, Ruth," Bess began. She sat down in a chair across from Ruth and looked at her. "How well do you remember names?"

"Fairly well," Ruth answered. "Why?"

"I just found out that our Chef had a grandmother here," Bess explained. "Her last name was Cordaro. She lived here years ago. Do you recall anyone with that name?"

"Well," Ruth began and she drew in her breath like she was filling her lungs with memories before speaking. "I do remember a Collette Cordaro. The last name was so unusual. She died two years ago. That's the only Cordaro I ever knew here. I think I recall her living here at that time. Collette was a lovely lady."

"Did you know her well?" Bess asked.

"No I didn't," Ruth quickly answered. "We never really talked all that much, though I saw her quite often in the hallways where we'd always exchange pleasant greetings. Oh, we'd make small talk after dinner but that was about it."

"I see," Bess nodded. "Do you remember if she had any regular visitors? Anyone she talked about who wasn't part of her family?"

"You know who I remember seeing her talk to a lot? Sister Francine," Ruth said.

"Who?" Bess asked.

"Collette was a Catholic," Ruth continued. "There was this nun...Sister Francine, who would come every

Sunday to visit with her. In fact, I still see Sister Francine here at the Honey Hills Center on Sundays. Of course, her hair is a little whiter…but she still takes the time to visit the residents from her church. Lovely lady. She wears a blue habit on her head and a matching blue dress. If you're ever near the sanctuary on Sundays…you'll see her."

Bess knew where the worship area was located. She would attend church every Sunday morning, as did most residents of Honey Hills. They were all at a point in their lives where the dust of a busy life had settled. There were no young children to tend, no jobs to perform, no bills to pay or groceries to buy. At this point in life, Bess thought, most everyone here was quite aware of their mortality. Church was the best remedy for easing one's fears of mortality. When Bess came to church, she had a favorite seat on the left hand side of the sanctuary, fourth row from the front. She found she had to sit closer so she could hear the sermon better. However, this Sunday morning was a little different. Bess chose to sit in the back of the church and felt badly about it because she wouldn't be able to hear the scripture readings nor the sermon. However, she told herself she was on an investigation. She wanted to have a clear view of the church so she could find the nun who had visited Mrs. Cordaro all those years ago.

"Bess?" Flo Morganstern said, pausing at the pew where Bess was sitting. "That's not your spot, Bess. Why are you sitting here? You usually sit up front."

"I've been running to the bathroom a good bit this morning," Bess fibbed and she rubbed her stomach to enhance her lie. "I don't trust sitting that far up."

Flo nodded and slowly made her way to her usual pew. Bess let out a sigh of relief and pondered what

Flo would do if she knew Bess was on the case about Tony the chef. Bess smiled when she thought about what Flo would say. While she smiled her eyes continued to glide over the many white heads that had gathered in the worship area before her. Then her eyes stopped on one head that didn't look white.

From where she was seated, Bess managed to spot what looked like a dark blue cloth being worn over the head of someone sitting towards the front of the church. Bess stood up and began to walk along the side aisle to her regular pew. While she walked, Bess kept one eye on the head that was wearing the blue cloth. She scanned the room, but only saw the white heads of residents. She quickly reasoned that this head with the blue cloth over it must belong to a nun.

Bess slid into her pew, just three rows back from who she believed was Sister Francine. She sat and turned her eyes to the main aisle where she saw the chaplain for the Honey Hills Center quietly walk to the front of the church. From the start of the service, through every hymn and every scripture reading, Bess kept one eye on the woman that she believed was Sister Francine. When the service was over, she saw the woman stand and turn around for the first time.

The smiling face of a woman filled Bess's view. The nun wore glasses that flashed in the light. White hair poked out from under the cloth she wore on her head. Her matching blue dress made her easy to pick out. Bess quickly stepped out of the pew when the service was over. She slipped through the crowd that was exiting the sanctuary, trying not to move too quickly towards the nun. At one point, Bess stood perfectly still and smiled to the person next to her while she watched the nun walk by. Bess turned and followed the nun out of the sanctuary and into the hallway. Bess carefully moved around the other residents in her attempt to catch up to the nun.

"Excuse me!" Bess called out, stepping around one person. She smiled when she saw the nun stop and turn in her direction. "Are you Sister Francine?"

The nun offered a measured smile to Bess. Even though she didn't know Bess, it appeared the nun was genuinely happy to be recognized.

"Yes I am," Sister Francine said, her head tipping to one side. "Do I know you?"

"Actually...I'm a friend of a friend," Bess answered and she took one small step closer to Sister Francine. "Collette Cordaro was my friend's name. She used to live here a few years ago. Do you remember Collette?"

"Why of course," Sister Francine nodded with a wide grin. "I remember Collette very well. It was a number of years ago...but I do remember visiting her. She was such a nice woman. A good soul that went straight to heaven...I'm sure."

"Yes," Bess nodded. "Good souls tend to do that. Sister, I would like to ask you about a ring that Collette was fond of wearing. It was a ring with a large diamond in it. Her mother gave it to her. It was said by a family member that the ring would sparkle nearly anywhere. You see the diamond in that ring was quite large and...well...I was curious about whether you recall seeing such a ring when you'd visit her?"

The smile slowly vanished from Sister Francine's face. Her eyes turned to the floor and she quietly nodded. Bess noticed how Sister Francine nervously grabbed the cross hanging around her neck and began to rub it with her thumb.

"You know when she died....they say that ring just...vanished," Bess said and she shook her head after the words. "It is hard for me to believe a ring that would sparkle so much could just disappear, Sister, but this one did. The family has looked for many years and still cannot find it. No one knows where it went. I am guessing you visited her many times, since I usually see you here on Sundays. Perhaps you stopped by to visit her on Sundays? On your visits, did Collette ever speak of someone who wanted to steal that ring? Did she ever speak of people who didn't like her? Can you think of anyone who may have had a reason to steal her diamond?"

Sister Francine remained silent and her one hand clutched the silver cross that hung around her neck. Judging by the tension in her hand, Bess could tell that the grip was a tight one.

"No," was all Sister Francine managed to say.

Bess looked at how she was clutching the cross. Her instincts were telling her something different than what this nun was saying. Perhaps, Bess thought, her instincts were off. After all, this woman was a nun. There was no reason for Bess's instincts to suspect a nun of theft. And yet, Bess wanted to hear more than one word in reply to her query.

"Well...thank you for answering my question," Bess said and she began to leave the sanctuary. As she walked out into the hallway she glanced back to see that Sister Francine hadn't moved from her spot.

"No!" Sister Francine said in a loud tone that echoed throughout the empty sanctuary. "It wasn't like that! It wasn't like that at all!"

Bess stepped back into the church. She walked down the aisle and stopped in front of Sister Francine, who was still standing in the aisle. She looked at Bess and began to nervously rub her silver cross with her thumb.

"Everyone loved Collette," Sister Francine quietly stated. "No one stole her ring."

"But it's gone," Bess sighed, taking a small step closer to Sister Francine. "What else could have happened to it, Sister? It vanished from her hand and it was never seen again. It must have been stolen."

"I know what happened to the ring," Sister Francine softly confessed. She pointed to a pew next to where they were standing. "Sit down with me. Let me tell you what happened."

THE RING

Together both ladies sat in the third pew from the front. Neither spoke. They watched a woman remove a colorful bouquet of flowers from one of the vases on the altar. When the woman left with the flowers, Bess found herself alone with Sister Francine. Sister Francine made the sign of the cross towards the front of the church. She turned to Bess and began to rub her thumb nervously over the cross that hung from her necklace.

"Let me begin by saying how good a person Collette Cordaro was," Sister Francine began. "It is important to understand that about Collette. She was a member of our church in her later years and when she moved here the church asked me to visit her."

"Why?" Bess asked.

"To offer communion and prayer," Sister Francine replied. "While the services here at the Honey Hills Center are lovely...they are not considered part of our denomination. With so many people coming here to church, the Center offers what I would call a middle of the road non-denominational service. They have no choice but to appease so many residents. However, that is why I was asked to visit Collette. There are other people I visit here, too. Collette was one of my favorites because of her sharp wit and her ability to see the bigger picture on issues."

"The bigger picture?" Bess asked.

"Let me describe Collette to you by her actions," Sister Francine explained. "When the church needed a new window after a severe storm, Collette was one of a few members of our congregation to organize a bake sale to raise money.   When an earthquake hit Mexico City, Collette led an effort to assemble packages of medical supplies to be shipped.   By Christmas she and some other ladies had packed and mailed one hundred boxes.   Collette was not the kind of person to worry about a broken window in her house…but she was the kind of person who would reach across the world to help others.   No one disliked Collette.   No one stole her ring."

"How can you be so sure?" Bess asked.

"Because she gave it to me," Sister Francine said, leaning closer to Bess and lowering her voice to a whisper.   "She wanted me to have it."

"You?" Bess said, her eyes glancing down at the nun's hands.

"A few years ago our church was involved with building a school in Haiti," Sister Francine began.   "We purchased uniforms for the children.   Taught them about math and God in the same day.   It was a Christian school and the children loved coming to it.   Then one day a large earthquake struck Haiti.   The country was reduced to rubble.   Our school was destroyed.   The day after the earthquake, when news spread of the devastation, our church thought it was important to rebuild the school…but the funds for doing so were quite limited."

"And you told Collette about this?" Bess asked.

"Collette led the original effort to build the school," Sister Francine explained.   "As I said, she was a special person and she reached across the world to help those young Haitian boys and girls so they could learn about God, and science, and math, and other things that children should know to help them escape such an impoverished life."

"So what happened to the ring?" Bess asked leaning back in her pew.

"I told Collette about the earthquake and the school," Sister Francine continued, "When I finished...well she told me right away about her ring. She spoke of its great value and then slipped it off her finger. She made me promise to use the ring to help rebuild the school."

"Do you have any proof of this?" Bess asked, careful not to sound like she was questioning Sister Francine's honesty. "I mean are there any documents you could share to substantiate the donation?"

"There's a record of her donation at my church," Sister Francine reported. "It's a notarized form. Of course, Collette died before I could give her a copy. I received the call about her death just a day after she gave me the ring. Of course, I wasn't quite sure how to share the news with her family about the ring."

"What do you mean?"

"They were grieving," Sister Francine recalled. "They were all so upset. I didn't have the chance to get their names, or write down phone numbers, or find any way of contacting them. All Collette said was how one daughter lived in Colorado and another daughter lived closer. I'm embarrassed for holding my silence...but Collette's gift has helped so many children."

Bess nodded at her words.

"The family must know the truth," Bess said and she stood up and rested her one hand on the pew in front of her. "We have a chef working in our kitchen here at the Honey Hills Center. His name is Tony. He is a very nice young man...right out of college. He was Collette's grandson. I would like you to tell him what you just told me."

"It was her dying wish," Sister Francine said. "How can I make a young man understand the importance of that?"

"I don't know," Bess replied. "I would urge you to come back here for dinner this evening. I will save a place for you at my table in the dining hall. When our meal is done, I will walk you back and introduce you to Tony. The rest, my dear, will be up to you."

Later that evening, after a dinner of chicken, rice and vegetables in a sauce that melted in her mouth, Bess and Sister Francine looked around at the other three ladies who shared the table. The newest member of the table, Minnie Darcy, cleared her throat and leaned close to Sister Francine.

"I don't get to church much since I moved here," Minnie confessed.

"A prayer every day to the good Lord would be enough," Sister Francine said. "You do pray, don't you?"

"Of course," Minnie answered. "I haven't been to confession in a long time, though."

"Is there anything you'd like to tell me?" Sister Francine asked. She rested her hand on Minnie's hand and smiled. "Have you committed any sins that are bothering you?"

"I stole a muffin," Minnie stated and her eyes glanced over at Bess. "It belonged to Bess and I took it when she wasn't looking. I apologized to Bess for what I did. I just…I wanted you to know what happened so you could pray for my forgiveness."

"Of course," Sister Francine said, gently patting Minnie's hand. "The Lord is very forgiving to those who ask for it."

"Thank you," Minnie said, leaning back in her seat.

Bess looked at Minnie then turned to Sister Francine. She couldn't believe that Minnie was still thinking about the muffin incident.

"Sister Francine," Bess finally said. "I think we should probably go. Are you finished?"

"Yes," Sister Francine nodded.

Together both women got up from the table and made their way across the dining room. Bess pushed open the door to the kitchen. Sister Francine followed her. Bess spotted Willie standing next to a sink, his arms buried deep in a large mound of white soap suds. He smiled at Bess while he lowered a dirty dish into the sink. Towards the back of the kitchen, surrounded by a pile of pots and pans, Bess spotted Chef Tony. Bess reached back and took Sister Francine by the hand. Together they moved around the stove and a cutting table. Chef Tony looked up and when he spotted Bess, he stopped gathering the dirty pots and pans.

"Tony," Bess began. "I'd like you to meet Sister Francine. She knew your grandmother quite well."

"Hello," Chef Tony said. "How did you know my grandma? Were you friends?"

"Yes we were," Sister Francine smiled. She reached out and shook Tony's hand.

"I believe you two have a lot to talk about," Bess said. She pointed to Tony's small enclosed office that was surrounded by windows. "Tony, if you want to take Sister Francine into your office, I can help Willie with the dishes."

"Very good of you, Mrs. Bullock," Sister Francine quickly said and she pointed across the kitchen to the office. "Let's go and talk about your grandmother, young man."

Bess watched them walk into Tony's office where he slowly closed the door behind them. Bess spun around and did a quick survey of the kitchen. Mounds of pots, pans and dishes could be spotted everywhere she turned. Then her eyes met Willie's and she took a deep breath.

"Well, Willie," Bess sighed, removing her sweater and carefully laying it down on a table. "I can see we have a lot of work to do. I guess we'd better get started."

For the next hour, Bess helped Willie clean every dirty pot, every stained pan and every soiled dish that could be found in the kitchen. The more dishes they washed the greater appreciation Bess developed for how much work Tony did in preparing three meals a day. While she helped Willie, Bess kept one eye on the windows that surrounded Chef Tony's office. She noticed that Sister Francine was doing most of the talking. Tony sat behind his desk and nodded his head every so often. On occasion, Bess could hear Tony's voice speak in short one or two word statements. The tone in his voice wasn't one of anger. In fact, Tony seemed very calm while Sister Francine explained the fate of his beloved grandmother's ring.

When Willie and Bess had finished the dishes, they moved on to sweeping up the kitchen floor. Willie carried out a few ingredients for tomorrow's breakfast. He laid out some cereal boxes on a side table, along with bowls and spoons.

"I think that does it for today, Mrs. Bullock," Willie announced.

"It's quite a job getting everything prepared for a meal," Bess observed.

"Things go easier when you're prepared," Willie said, looking out at the dining room. "That's what Tony says and I think he's right."

Willie turned out a light and the kitchen became quite dim. He opened the door to the dining room and waited for Bess to leave. Bess turned to see that Tony's office was still well lit. Through the office window she could still see Tony and Sister Francine sitting by his desk. They were now smiling about something. Bess managed to catch Sister Francine's eye. In that second, Sister Francine smiled and nodded to Bess, then quickly resumed her conversation. With the long shadows of the kitchen gathered around her, Bess quietly stepped through the door and followed Willie out of the dining room.

HOW TO SHARE A CHET

With so much of her time being focused on Chef Tony and Willie, Bess accidently missed the last meeting of the Waltzing Club. While she enjoyed not thinking about her problems with Lillian, she missed Chet and was anxious to attend the next meeting. On the morning of Waltzing Club, Bess checked her watch more than once before heading out the door. When she arrived for the meeting, Bess was surprised to find Lillian standing in front of Chet, chatting with him about something. Bess took a deep breath and smiled at the other members of the club who were present. She said hello to a few friends, but found that her eyes kept returning to Chet and Lillian. Finally, Bess stepped to the back of the group and allowed her eyes to settle on Chet and Lillian.

"Okay, everyone," Chet announced and he clapped twice so all conversations stopped and all eyes were on him. "We have a new dance step this morning. Bess, if you could come here I'll show everyone what kind of dance it will be."

"Chet?" Lillian spoke up. "I'm standing right here. Why don't you let me be your partner? You did last week. Besides, poor Bess is all the way back there."

Chet's eyes looked to the back of the room. Bess nodded in approval. She watched Chet take Lillian's hand and together they demonstrated a new dance for the club. Bess told herself she didn't own Chet. He was free to dance with whomever he wanted, even Lillian.

"We swing to the left," Chet announced while he and Lillian moved. "Two steps this way…two steps that way…kick once and turn."

Bess could feel her face grow red while she watched them dance.

"He's not yours….he is not yours…" Bess whispered over and over to herself.

The more she said it the more she could feel her heart begin to ache. What were her instincts trying to tell her about Chet? At first, she thought they were her investigative instincts at work, conveying suspicions about Lillian. However, Bess soon realized these instincts were altogether different. They were instincts of her heart, not of her mind. It had been so long since she felt romantic instincts like this, she barely recognized them. Bess drew in her breath, turned and walked out of the room. She began to walk down the hall and she could feel her eyes start to well up with tears. She wiped them with the back of her hand, conscious of a nurse who walked by her.

"Bess!" she heard a man's voice call out.

Bess stopped and turned back to see Chet quickly moving down the hallway after her.

She stopped and watched him rush down the hall. His eyes were wide and his eyebrows went up to form a look of surprise and concern. His mouth hung open like he knew what he was going to say the second he got to her.

"Bess!" Chet said when he reached her. "What's wrong? Are you okay?"

"It's nothing," Bess said with a wave of her hand.

"Something is wrong," Chet asked, stepping closer to her. "I can see the tears on your face. Please…tell me."

"It's just about our dance club," Bess said with a half-laugh. She shook her head at the ridiculous nature of what she was about to say. "I realize you're...I mean we...are not committed to each other. We are free to date anyone. However, I have noticed the way Lillian is throwing herself at you at our meetings."

"Lillian?" Chet laughed and he shook his head after his reply.

"She has told me as much," Bess nodded. "She said that men like women who need help every now and then. Now if that's true...then maybe I'm not the kind of person you are looking for, Chet. I love being with you on the dance floor and on our walks...but if I'm not the right woman for you ...I hope you would tell me."

Chet smiled at her words.

"Why are you smiling?" Bess asked. "Please tell me what you're thinking."

Chet raised his hands and gently pressed the palms of his hands on her cheeks. His hands were warm and soft. Bess could feel her eyes blinking faster, which surprised her.

"I've never seen you so...undone," Chet stated. He leaned close and softly kissed her lips for the second time since she knew him. When he slowly pulled his lips away he smiled.

"I...I'm sorry," Bess said, nervously adjusting her hair. "I don't know what's come over me. I guess...I think...well...I think it must be...love."

Chet leaned in one more time and gave her a soft warm kiss on the cheek.

"It's love for me too, Bess," Chet announced. "Lillian can ask me for all the help she wants...but it won't change my feelings for you. Maybe we should do something so Lillian knows how I feel about you."

"Do something?" Bess asked.

"Yes," Chet replied. "I noticed that house that we walk by every morning, the one with the two gardens in the backyard. Well, I learned that the house is still available. We could inquire about getting it, Bess. Of course, we'd need to get married to make it proper. That is…if you want to get married. What do you say, Bess? Would you consider marrying me?"

Bess covered her mouth with her hand. She could feel a smile form behind her fingers. The pain and jealousy in her heart quickly drained away. In its place, a kind of giddiness she hadn't felt since she was a school girl. Bess grinned and tried to control the feelings that were coursing through her. She knew this was a big decision and she wanted to wait for her emotions to calm before she made a decision.

"Give me some time to think about it," Bess managed to say and she finished her thought with a kiss on Chet's cheek.

PROPOSAL

Later that night Bess found it difficult to sleep. The proposal from Chet rang in her mind and made it hard for her to think about anything else. It also rekindled memories that flashed in her mind, memories of a much younger Bess rejecting her late husband's first proposal out of fear more than anything else. Bess could recall how hard it was for her to trust people when she was younger. After turning down his first proposal, Bess's husband waited a full year before he asked her again. She accepted his second proposal for marriage without hesitation. Now eighty years old, she had no intentions of turning Chet down while secretly hoping for him to propose again. She promised to give him an answer in the morning. She promised to think about his proposal and that was what she went to bed fully intending to do. Yet, when she turned off the light, and thought about her options, Bess immediately turned on her light again.

She sat up in bed, pushed down her sheets, and turned herself around so she was sitting in her bed. She sat up, slid her legs off the side of the bed and let her feet dangle for a moment like a school girl. Her eyes turned to a small picture frame sitting on her nightstand. Her husband's face beamed at her from the frame.

"What do you think?" Bess quietly asked the picture.

Her husband's face merely grinned in silent reply.

"I do love you," Bess sighed to the picture. She held her ring finger with her other hand and rubbed the wedding band with her thumb. "I...I've met this person, you see. He's someone who makes me feel the way you used to. I've missed that feeling for nearly half my life. Now that I have it...I just don't want to lose it again. Do you understand?"

The picture remained silent and the face simply smiled at her. She shook her head and tucked her feet into her slippers. Bess stood up, hearing the familiar sounds of both knees crack as they did every morning she rose. She grabbed her robe and headed for the door.

It was not that unusual for residents of the Honey Hills Center to walk the hallways in their robes. Some were heading for a bath. Others were merely on the way to or from the dining room for a quick snack before bed. However, Bess knew the hour was late. The clock in her room told her it was well past midnight.

When she stepped into the hallway, Bess noticed how only a few of the lights were on. This was usually done during overnight hours, though Bess could only guess to save money. She looked up and down the dimly lit hall, but didn't see a soul. Given the late time of the night, a vacant hall didn't surprise Bess all that much. She tightened the sash on her robe and began to walk and think about the possibilities of being married again.

She did love Chet. He made her feel things she hadn't felt since her dear husband was alive. The idea of sharing a life with someone like Chet simply made Bess smile. She also loved the idea of moving back into a regular home. However, it wasn't just the home, but the two gardens in the backyard, too. While it had only been a couple years since she left her home and her gardens, Bess often thought it seemed like a lifetime ago since she could pick and choose flowers and vegetables to plant in a garden. Those were some of many good reasons to say "yes" to Chet's proposal.

When she thought about the negatives, the first picture that appeared in her mind was her daughter's face. Samantha's reaction to her mother's news would be mixed. Samantha was fully grown and a mother herself. She was also divorced and wasn't the biggest champion for the institution of marriage. The faces of her Bridge Club friends also poured into Bess's mind. It would be hard not to see them in the hallways if she moved away. Bess wasn't sure how married life would change her Bridge Club routine. The thought brought up another concern for Bess, the challenge that came with change.

She liked having quiet time in her room to sit and think about things. Would Chet keep her too busy? Would he give her the time she needed to sit, soak up the silence and think about things? Would her days change drastically or stay the same?

Bess pondered all of these thoughts while she shuffled down an empty hallway in her robe and slippers. She turned a corner and came to an open sitting area with a fish tank in the middle of the room. She sat down on one of the couches and stared at the fish. Bess marveled at how gracefully the fish could swim around each other while sharing such a small tank. As she pondered the question of marriage, her eyes followed a gold fish that curved and swerved in and around the bubbles. Just above the glass case, Bess noticed a small gold plate on the top of the tank. She had been in this sitting room many times before, but she never really noticed the gold plate on the top of the tank.

Bess stood up and walked over to examine the inscription on the golden plate. Screwed into the top of the tank, the rectangular shaped plate contained ten small words. Bess leaned over and softly read the words to herself.

For my dear wife Agnes, from her loving husband Clark."

Bess smiled and stared at the words. Only the soft sounds of the aquarium filled the moment. Bess stepped back and took a good look at the fish. They were here, she told herself, swimming in front of her because of love. The aquarium was here because of one man's love for his wife. It was something that most people at the Honey Hills Center enjoyed looking at a few times a day. It was something that brought people pleasure when they watched the fish. It was something that was here because of the love of one person for another.

The revelation caused Bess to think about the things in her life that were a product of love. Her daughter, Samantha. Her granddaughter, Nicole. The memories of her marriage. The best things in her life were things that came to her because of love. Perhaps, Bess told herself, good things would come again from her love for Chet.

In her mind, she could see herself walking outside with Chet. She could see him holding her hand as they stood and admired her gardens at sunset. The image was so clear she could almost smell the flowers. She could see her white hair spinning over her shoulder from a puff of wind. She could see the easy way that she and Chet smiled and chatted about things. The more she entertained the picture of her and Chet the more her heart ached for it all to be real. Her heart longed for this day, when she would truly be able to stand in *their* backyard, next to *her* flowers, and hold the hand of the man she loved.

All good things came from love, Bess thought. At the moment, love was giving Bess an answer to Chet's proposal. An answer that she hoped would lead to more good things in her life. Still there was something that didn't feel quite right. While her heart was committed to love, her mind was still having doubts. She had been married before and she needed to address that matter. Was her heart big enough to hold feelings for two husbands? She knew of one person that she could talk to about such matters.

ADVICE AFTER CARDS

"He asked me to marry him."

The words Bess spoke seemed to drown in the silence of the book room. No one was looking at their cards, or the table, or even speaking about the game of Bridge. All eyes were on Bess. The faces of her friends seemed to be frozen by what she told them. She was hoping to receive some kind of congratulations, or some laughter, or some kind of positive response to her news. Instead her three best friends looked at her with expressionless faces.

"Well," Flo finally spoke. "I guess you took care of that Lillian Peck problem."

"Bess," Alma Crisp chimed in. "Did he really ask you to marry him?"

"Yes," Bess answered. "Well, Chet and I have been together for almost a year. Then there's a house along Dogwood Lane that we've both had our eye on. I think our love and the house were factors in leading us to talk about marriage."

"Not to mention that man hunter Lillian Peck," Flo added.

"Yes, her too," Bess acknowledged.

"So are you going to move into the house?" Rose asked.

"We would like to," Bess answered.

"And what about Bridge Club?" Flo asked. "How will you get to Bridge Club if you're living all the way over on Dogwood Lane?"

"I'll walk I guess," Bess answered.

"It gets mighty cold in the winter for walking," Flo pressed. "You say that now when it's nice…but when there's snow on the ground you'll leave us one player short and skip Bridge Club. We can't play Bridge with three players, Bess."

"Don't worry, Flo," Bess calmly stated with a wave of her hand. "I'll always be sitting with you ladies on a Tuesday morning…no matter where I live."

"So what are you going to tell him?" Alma asked. Alma was the romantic of the group and often spoke about the latest romance novel she'd read. "I think it is so wonderful to hear about someone finding love so late in life. What will your answer be, Bess?"

"I'm not sure," Bess answered. "Having been married before…it's all a bit complicated for me. I mean…Chet's a good man…but I was already married to a good man once in my life. As I said, it's all a bit complicated. I'll have to figure it out. Now we all didn't come here to listen to me. We came to play cards."

"We can do both," Alma grinned.

"I'd rather just play," Flo said, tapping her cards on the table.

"Congratulations, Bess," Rose whispered.

With the consistency of a reliable clock, all four ladies looked down at their cards, one card was played, and the rhythm of the game resumed right where it had left off when Bess announced her news.

Soon another Tuesday morning of Bridge Club was completed. Bess lingered afterwards and said goodbye to Alma Crisp and Flo Morgenstern. Alma hugged Bess and congratulated her again on the engagement. Bess smiled and watched Alma and Flo make their way out of the book room. Bess turned to Rose Grumbine, who had finished packing the playing cards into a box.

When she stood up to leave, Bess quickly grabbed Rose by the arm.

"Rose," Bess began. "Can I speak with you before you go?"

"Of course, Bess," Rose replied and she pointed to the doorway. "I was just going to stop at the greenhouse to check on some flowers. Walk along with me and we can talk while I water my plants."

The Honey Hills's greenhouse was actually a modestly sized room connected to the eastern side of the center. It had a glass roof and large windows that filled the room with morning sun. Any resident could put a potted plant on one of the tables in the room for the winter and nurture its growth until the spring. Rose had a strong passion for flowers. Both of her parents were florists, which was a factor in deciding her first name. They also conveyed to Rose their love for all plants and flowers. Every winter, Bess thought Rose kept more plants and flowers in the greenhouse than anyone else at the Honey Hills Center. Now that spring was here, it was time for Rose to begin the process of relocating her many plants and flowers outside.

"Look at this," Rose said, waving Bess to a table.

Bess stepped over to Rose where she found a dull orange pot on the table and a large bag of potting soil on the floor next to the table. The air smelled like soil and the morning sun made the room feel quite warm. Rose pointed to a delicate purple flower growing from the soil in the pot and smiled like she had been a lucky hunter capturing something rare and elusive.

"What is it?" Bess asked, leaning her head over the pot.

"It's an orchid," Rose announced. "They're quite hard to grow over the winter. Now that spring is here, I have to find a spot outside to move it."

"I see," Bess nodded. She took a step closer to Rose and cleared her throat. "Rose...I have something to ask you? It's about Chet's proposal."

"Yes, that is good news about you two," Rose grinned. "Congratulations, Bess. I guess you took care of that Lillian problem after all."

"Yes," Bess answered with a slight smile. "You see, Rose, I was quite surprised when Chet asked me to marry him.   I   mean...I'm   happy   about   his proposal...but I still keep a picture of my husband in my room. I look at him every night before I go to sleep. Some nights...when I can't sleep...I stare at his face and I feel a real comfort come over me. I know you've been married twice, Rose. How did you manage to sort out your feelings for your first husband with those for your second husband?"

Rose sniffed at her orchid, then put the pot down and remained silent. Rose was always a bit thoughtful before she spoke. It was a quality Bess liked about Rose, so she was patient in waiting for an answer and this was one of those times.

"When my first husband died," Rose finally began, "I was quite young. You know...when you're young you feel quite strongly about things. My feelings for Charlie were very passionate ones. He was my young love...and then he was gone. Years later when I married again...it was a different kind of love. I was older and so was Carl, my second husband. Our love was formed more out of friendship and companionship. It was the kind of love that comes from holding hands, laughing together, and caring for each other. Young love involves emotions...but it also involves more physical affection, too. For me, that was a clear distinction between the two loves of my life. They came at two different periods in my life...and I always felt like the young woman I was had a perfect match and then the older woman I became was also lucky to have found another perfect match. I was very fortunate to have found two loves in my life, Bess. Now you are just as lucky."

Bess simply nodded at Rose's words. Rose was right about how she looked at her two husbands. When Bess was a young mother caring for Samantha, her husband was a perfect match. He was young and handsome. He worked hard and loved Bess with all of his heart. When he came home from work, he would slip his hands around her waist and kiss her on the back of the neck. It was the tingle of that kiss that made Bess giggle at least once a day. At night, when Samantha was asleep, Bess and her husband would share their passion in ways like most other young couples.

What made her happy now? Bess thought for a moment about this question. It wasn't a kiss anymore. It wasn't the idea of physical passion. What put a smile on her face was Chet looking at her. Watching Chet smile. The feeling of Chet's soft warm hand wrapping around her fingers when they walked. Dancing with Chet and looking into his blue eyes. At this point in her life, she didn't need a kiss on the neck or a tingle down her back. She needed a companion. She needed good conversation. She needed someone to walk with, hold her hand, and tell her how much she was loved. These were the things that were most important at this time in her life. Eighty years old was very different from twenty years old, Bess thought.

After talking to Rose, Bess now knew that it was a miracle that she found someone at this point in her life...someone who loved her...someone who wanted to spend the rest of his life with her. It was a miracle. Bess now knew that she had to embrace this miracle.

YOUTH AND PASSION

After a Tuesday morning meeting of Bridge Club, Bess took her time leaving the book room. She wanted to savor the good feelings she had from chatting, laughing, and playing Bridge with her friends. She stayed seated and watched her friends begin to prepare to leave in their usual order.

Rose was typically the first to go, mumbling something about a hair appointment and quickly checking her watch. Alma usually followed close behind. This morning Alma mentioned that she had a niece coming to visit her. Flo was always the last one to leave. Most Tuesday mornings, Flo lingered at the table, packing up the deck of cards, pushing in chairs, and cleaning up any stray hard candy wrappers on the table or floor.

This morning, Bess stayed behind to help Flo clean up the room. After moving the last chair, Bess turned to the many books that lined the walls of the book room. She walked around and took the time to look at a few of the titles printed along the bindings. Some of the bindings were cracked, making the letters hard to read. She reached out and rolled her fingers along the spines of the books, noting the different textures. Then she stopped and looked down.

A thick maroon colored book was lying on the floor. She bent down to pick up the book with one hand, but the weight of the book caused her arthritis to flare up. She dropped the book and winced at the pain in her fingers. When the book hit the floor, Bess saw something fall out from between the pages. It was a small white envelope.

"Well look at that," Bess sighed.

"What?" Flo asked, looking up from the table. She pointed at the envelope on the floor. "Where did that envelope come from? Is there anything in it?"

"I'm not quite sure," Bess answered.

She picked up the envelope, opened it and found a slip of paper inside. She carefully pulled out the paper and unfolded it. Bess scanned the small curves and slopes of writing that made up the letter. After reading it, Bess took a deep breath, held the letter close to her face and began to re-read the words to herself again.

My Love,

The war rages on but you are not far from my thoughts. My heart aches for you every day and I can't wait to hold you in my arms, feel your soft hair on my cheek, and breath in your sweetness. At night, when the gunfire is silent, I look up at the stars and think about you star gazing too. The moon and the stars are where our eyes can meet every night and the peace of heaven is what our hearts can share. When this war is over, I long for the day to come home, hold you close and whisper the words that my heart aches to tell you. My heart flies when I imagine touching you. You are my flower, my sweet, my love. As my favorite writer would say, "believe me, my love, you are as fair as any mother's child and your beauty as bright as those gold candles fixed in heaven's air."

All my love,

Trent

Bess felt her eyes welling up. She read the note again and then slipped the letter back into the envelope.

She looked down at the thick book on the floor. Bess carefully reached down with both hands, picked up the book and placed it on a table. She studied the bright gold letters that were etched into the leather cover of the book.

"*The Love Sonnets of William Shakespeare*," Bess read.

"What did you say?" Flo asked, walking up beside Bess.

"It's the title of this book," Bess explained, tapping the cover of the book with her fingers. She held up the envelope. "You see, I found a book on the floor. When I picked it up, this fell out."

"What's in the envelope?" Flo asked.

"The most beautiful letter I've ever read," Bess said, handing the envelope over to Flo. "It's from a young man who I believe used to be a soldier. It appears he was writing to his wife during some war. Oh, Flo, it just moved me to tears reading the words he wrote."

"Let me see," Flo said and she pulled the letter out of the envelope.

"They are words from a young heart," Bess explained. "Words that are filled with the kind of passion one writes with when one is young. That's what I feel when I read this letter. I am quite certain that whoever this belongs to will want it back. I mean, what kind of wife wouldn't want her husband's love letter. Especially one like this. Clearly it was left in this book by mistake."

"Yes, it's very nice," Flo mumbled, folding the letter back up and passing it to Bess. "There's no last name on the envelope. How will you know who it belongs to? Maybe the book was donated to Honey Hills. You know a lot of the books in this book room were donated.

That letter might not even belong to someone who lives here."

"You may be right," Bess nodded. "I did find the book on the floor, though. An envelope this big would have stuck out of the top of the pages. I believe someone would have noticed if the book had been donated. I'd be willing to guess that this book was being read by someone who lives here. Perhaps they were using the envelope as some kind of bookmark and simply forgot about it. I just need to find that person and return this letter to them."

"But how?" Flo asked. She waved her hand at the book on the table. "Just leave it there with the book, Bess. Whoever lost it will come back for it. C'mon, it's almost time for lunch. I heard Chef Tony is making some kind of minestrone soup. I'm sure it will be delicious and I don't want to miss it."

"You go ahead," Bess said with a wave of her hand. "I'm going to stay here for a bit."

"Suit yourself," Flo said and she quickly exited the book room.

Even though Bess could feel her stomach growl in disagreement, she felt compelled to find the owner of the letter. Bess settled into the fluffy blue couch in the center of the room. She held the book on her lap, turned her eyes to the door and waited. Would the person come back for the letter? If not, how would she track the person down? The only clue to this mystery was the book on her lap. It was quite clear to her that someone had been reading the book and accidently left the letter inside. Her thoughts then drifted to the letter.

What was the story behind the letter? Who was Trent? Her husband served in the war, but he never wrote her such letters filled with so much passion. In fact, Bess recalled that he never could express his feelings for her in a way that moved her to tears. What would it be like to be married to such a man? How many years would this kind of passion last in a marriage? After sorting out her thoughts, Bess felt more determined to find the owner of the letter. While she contemplated her plan for investigating, she crossed one leg, adjusted her glasses and began to read some of the love sonnets of William Shakespeare. Every so often, her eyes would drift over to an open door and a doorway that remained empty for most of the afternoon.

THE NECESSITY FOR ATTENTION

She took the book with her and carried it around for the rest of the day. After dinner, she sat by herself at her table sipping coffee as she often did at the end of the day. The book sat on the table directly in front of her. She stared down at the cover of the book, and the envelope that stuck out from the pages. As the ladies filed out of the dining room, a few commented on the book and smiled at Bess. No one stopped to claim the book. No one inquired about a letter that had been accidently left between the pages. Once every person had left the dining room, Bess sipped on the last half of her warm coffee and pondered her investigation.

How would she find the owner of this letter? Bess assumed the letter belonged to a resident of the Honey Hills Center. If so, how would Bess manage to find the person? There were many residents of Honey Hills. The challenge to this investigation was becoming quite clear to Bess. While most of her other mysteries required her to be subtle, to blend in, and to observe others, this case would be altogether different. It was going to be a case that would require Bess to stand out. It would require her to draw attention to herself and the book that she would have to keep with her. She thought it was almost like she was going to keep the book hostage until the right person stepped forward. She rested her hand on the cover of the book and made a promise to herself. Whether it would take days or weeks, Bess would not return the book to the book room until someone came to her to ask for the letter.

Bess drank the last of her coffee, stood up, and smiled at Willie who was coming over to her table.

"May I take these things?" Willie asked, gesturing to her dishes and utensils.

"Everything but the book," Bess replied and she handed him her coffee cup. She watched him take her plate, her utensils, and her napkin. When he walked away, Bess scooped up the book with both hands. She smiled at the book. "I'm afraid we're going to be spending a lot of time together."

The next day, Bess knew what she would do the moment she got awake. Once dressed, she carried the book down to the dining hall and chatted with some friends before sitting down to prepare her breakfast. She spoke quite loudly to the ladies at her table about how much she was enjoying *Shakespeare's Love Sonnets.* When she left the dining hall, Bess carried the book by her side so that every table could see what she was reading.

Instead of taking her morning walk outside with Chet, Bess decided to take a walk around the hallways of Honey Hills by herself. As in the dining hall, she made certain to keep the book by her side while she walked. If anyone spoke to Bess, she was mindful to bring Shakespeare's *Love Sonnets* into the conversation. When she grew tired of walking, Bess sat in a chair and read a little, being mindful to keep the cover of the book held up for those passing by to see. During the middle of the afternoon, Bess began to notice that there were fewer residents than usual sitting in an open area of the Center. It was a large room with a television mounted on the wall and various couches and chair scattered around it. However, Bess found that she was the only person seated in the room. Bess spied a nurse walking down the hallway.

"Where is everyone?" Bess called out to the nurse.

"There's a concert in the chapel," the nurse replied. "A local college has brought a string quartet in to play. They've been here before and everyone quite enjoys their music. I think the concert just started...if you'd like to go."

"Did you say it's in the chapel?" Bess asked for clarification.

"Yes," the young nurse replied.

Bess quickly walked away. She held the book by her side and made a brisk walk to the chapel. Once there, she meandered up and down the main aisle of the chapel, slowly turning and pretending to look for a seat. When she found a pew to sit in, Bess was careful to lift the book high in the air while she stepped around one woman who refused to give up her aisle seat.

When she sat down to listen to the music, Bess couldn't help but wonder how many ladies were present for the concert. She turned her eyes and combed over the many faces seated behind her. She wondered if one of the ladies in attendance was the one who would recognize the book. Bess sat back in her seat and listened to the two violins and the harp performing up front. The sweet melodies that filled the air caused Bess to relax for a few minutes and enjoy the sounds. The music put her in the mind of spring; colorful tulips, bright red cardinals and trees filled with snowy white cherry blossoms.

Soon the performance was over and applause filled the sanctuary. Bess was the first one to stand up. When she turned to leave, she paused in front of each pew to let people out. Bess smiled at each person who passed in front of her. She cradled the book in her arm like a baby and watched the eyes of the people leaving the pews. Bess noted how their eyes would move from her face, to the book, then to the floor before stepping into the aisle to leave. It was a good place to be to be seen with the book. Bess couldn't count all the faces, but there were a good many of them who now knew she had the book.

She spent the rest of the day in the hallways, sitting in her room with her door open, and even lingering in the book room. Wherever she went, the book of *Shakespeare's Sonnets* was always at Bess's side. When it was lunch time, she returned to the dining hall with the book. When she put the book down on the table, Clara Carson looked across the table at Bess and smiled.

"You sure must like that book, Bess," Clara observed.

"I guess I do," Bess laughed.

By the end of the day, Bess sat in her room resting her right arm on a pillow on her lap. She was not used to carrying something so heavy for the course of a day. It reminded Bess of how she felt as a young mother, carrying her daughter, Samantha, around the house for a day. She then began to ponder which was heavier, the book or baby Samantha. Bess took a deep breath and focused on the book on her lap. She slid the envelope out from the book and read the letter again. Had she taken the wrong approach to this investigation? Did her instincts lead her to a case without resolution? Bess drew in her breath, surveyed the darkness gathering outside her window and began to dress for bed. While she dressed she began to harbor some doubts about whether this would indeed be a mystery she would be able to solve.

TIME FOR NICOLE

Nicole was coming. The mere thought of these three words caused a broad smile to fill Bess's face. Nicole was her granddaughter, a precocious seven year old who had a head full of brown curls and big brown eyes that Bess could never say "no" to. However, as Bess often told herself, grandmothers weren't supposed to say "no" to their grandchildren. Given Nicole's circumstances, Bess always found it hard to say anything other than "yes" to her wishes.

Nicole was an only child. Her parents were divorced, but she lived with her mother, Samantha. While Bess was quite happy that her daughter had full custody of Nicole, the situation was still quite sad. Bess's former son-in-law now lived and worked on the other side of the country in Seattle, Washington. Like her mother, Nicole's father was also an only child. The result was that Samantha was the loneliest child in the world, or so Bess thought. Nicole had no cousins, no siblings, and no father. With the exception of her mother, Nicole's only extended family was Bess. Thus, whenever Nicole asked to spend the day with Bess, she was quick to grant her granddaughter's wish. While Bess was aware of her limited resources at the Honey Hills Center, she always managed to find enough activities to keep Nicole busy. Bess reviewed the events in her head while she stood by the parking lot waiting for her daughter's car to arrive. Almost on cue, a bright red car accelerated through the parking lot and pulled right up to the curb where the main entrance to

the Honey Hills Center was located. Bess watched a
car door fly open and Nicole jumped out.

"Nana!" Nicole chirped when she hopped out of
the back seat. A wide smile filled Nicole's face. She
grabbed her pink backpack from her mother, sprinted
for Bess and dove into her arms.

"Hello, my love," Bess said, giving Nicole a big
hug and a kiss on the head. Her hair smelled like
strawberries and her hug was warm.

"I'll pick her up around four, Mom," Samantha
said, glancing at her cell phone as if she were talking to
it instead of Bess. "I have some work to do in the
office and then I'll be back. Are you sure you're okay
with this? I could get a sitter to watch Nicole since
she's off from school today."

"No need for a babysitter," Bess grinned and she
ran her fingers through Nicole's curls. "We need a
little Bullock girl time today...don't we, Nicole?"

Nicole simply giggled in agreement.

From the second Samantha drove away, Bess and
Nicole began to make a day of it. The morning began
with a trip to the beauty salon that was located in the
Honey Hills Center. Bess had called the day before and
made reservations for her and Nicole. By ten o'clock
grandmother and granddaughter were getting their hair
washed and dried. Nicole enjoyed the old fashioned
hair dryer that fit over her head and blew warm air
down over her hair and face. She sat in a chair next to
Bess where they both enjoyed reading while their hair
dryers hummed softly in their ears. Bess indulged in
reading newspapers that contained articles on what was
happening in the world. Nicole had brought some
chapter books in her backpack and was content reading
one of them while her hair dried.

After the hair appointment, Bess and Nicole swung by to visit Alma Crisp. Nicole loved to look at Alma's brightly colored clothes. Bess and Alma sat on the bed and chatted while Nicole dove into Alma's closet and giggled at some of the fancy tops and colorful shoes she found. Alma was always a snappy dresser and Nicole liked her for it. Alma even got out some of her fanciest silk scarves to try on Nicole. Bess laughed as she watched Alma wrap one scarf after another around Nicole's neck. Bess couldn't tell who was having more fun. Nicole clearly enjoyed being fussed over and Alma enjoyed having a young girl to dress up. In some ways, Bess thought, the concept of dress-up was something that stayed with Alma all her life. While Nicole wasn't a doll, she might as well be, Bess thought.

Soon it was time for lunch. Bess grabbed an extra chair and the other ladies who shared Bess's table were more than happy to make room for Nicole. It was nice to see smiles on the faces of everyone who shared Bess's table. A few of the ladies asked Nicole questions about school, about her friends, and Nicole spoke quite loudly about her favorite TV shows. Bess noted how everyone at the table beamed when they listened to Nicole speak. Her voice was filled with a combination of hope and innocence that Bess thought the other ladies enjoyed. Residents at the Honey Hills Center were more inclined to talk about their ailments, their medications, and their memories. It was quite pleasing to hear a young girl speak about her friends, her favorite ice cream flavors and her favorite pet that she hoped to get one day.

Later in the afternoon, Bess and Nicole were going to join Flo Morgenstern for a game of Bingo that was being organized in the dining hall.

"Now you know Flo likes to win," Bess advised Nicole as they sat in Bess's room . "You may not want to talk to her that much when she plays, Nicole. She takes Bingo very seriously."

"I remember," Nicole sighed. "One time I told Flo how I cry when I lose a game of four square at school. I told her how the bigger girls...sometimes they just hit the ball too hard for me. Flo told me to get mean and hit the ball harder than the other girls. She was right cuz now I win a lot more at four square."

"I see," Bess nodded. "Well...Flo she doesn't like to lose."

"No one likes to lose," a voice spoke from the doorway.

Bess looked up from Nicole's face to find Flo standing by the door. In her hands, Bess spotted a stack of Bingo cards and a plastic container of Bingo chips. Flo always brought her own cards and Bingo chips, even though they were provided. Flo insisted that her cards and chips brought her luck.

"Hi, Flo," Nicole said and she quickly ran over and gave Flo a hug.

"Hello, Nicole," Flo said and she looked down at Nicole hugging her and smiled at Bess. "Getting hugged by you, Nicole...well, it's like getting hit with a warm breeze."

"Nicole gives good hugs," Bess smiled.

"Now tell me about four square," Flo began. "Are you winning more?"

As she watched Nicole talk to Flo about four square, Bess noticed a small woman appear in the hallway behind Flo. The woman lingered in the hall, not moving down the hallway and not retreating back up the hall. Bess noticed how the woman was trying to peek into her room, moving her head to look around Flo and Nicole.

"Excuse me!" Bess finally called out and she stepped closer to the door. "This nice lady is standing behind you, Flo. I was just curious to know what she needed. Can I help you?"

When Flo moved to the side, Bess found a slight woman with short gray hair that was arranged into tight curls. She adjusted her glasses and stepped around Flo and Nicole. She was shorter than Flo and barely taller than Nicole. The small woman made eye contact with Bess.

"My name is Evelyn Short," the woman announced. "Are you Bess Bullock?"

"I am," Bess replied.

"I've seen you in the hallways," Evelyn explained. She pointed at the book on Bess's nightstand. "You've been carrying that book around with you for days. It's a book about poems written by Shakespeare. I've been waiting for you to return the book to the book room so I may borrow it. You see I had borrowed that book a few days ago...right before you.... and I need it back, Mrs. Bullock."

"Well I'm afraid I'm not finished with it yet," Bess said, scooping up the book from her nightstand and placing it on her lap. She tapped the cover with her hand. "As you well know, it is a very thick book. It's taking me a long time to read but I'm quite enjoying it. I haven't read Shakespeare since I was in college. Despite my age, I find that Shakespeare still takes me a long time to read. It is just as challenging as it was in college...but still worth it."

"I really must look inside that book," Evelyn pressed, taking a step closer to Bess.

Out of the corner of her eye, Bess managed to see Nicole standing in front of Flo.

Nicole's eyes were quite big. The expression on her face told Bess she was concerned about what was happening. Bess looked at Flo, who also appeared to be curious over what would transpire between Bess and Evelyn.

"Flo," Bess began. "Would you take Nicole to the dining hall for Bingo? I'll be along in a little while."

"Are you okay being by yourself?" Flo asked, her eyes shifting to Evelyn.

"Yes," Bess replied without hesitation. "Mrs. Short and I are just fine. Please save me a seat and I will be down soon."

Flo took Nicole by the hand and Bess watched them vanish into the hallway. Bess now focused on Evelyn. She waved her to a chair next to where Bess was sitting.

"Sit down, my dear," Bess said. "I think I know why you want this book and I suspect it's not for the sonnets."

Bess reached into the cover of the book and slowly pulled out the envelope that contained the letter. She handed the envelope to Evelyn, who quickly opened it and pulled out the letter. She unfolded the slip of paper and her eyes began to dart from side to side, as if checking to see if any words were missing or if any letters had magically vanished. When she was finished reading, a small distinct smile appeared on her face.

"A letter that special should not be left in a book, my dear," Bess observed.

"I have my reasons for leaving it there," Evelyn whispered, putting the letter back in the envelope.

"The words in that letter just brought my heart to life," Bess said, pointing at the envelope. "It made me feel things I haven't felt since I was a girl. It reminded me of...young love. Hopeful love. Passionate love. Tell me, Evelyn, what was it like to know someone like this? What was it like to share a love with someone who was so clearly passionate?"

Evelyn looked down at the letter on her lap. She smoothed her hand over the paper envelope and sighed. She looked at Bess and uttered three simple words,
"I don't know."

EVELYN AND THE LETTER

"You don't know?" Bess asked and she leaned her head forward slightly. "I thought this was a letter written by your husband?"

"No," Evelyn replied. She paused for a moment, cleared her throat, and held the envelope in the air. "This letter was written to me around the time our country was fighting in a war. You see, the boys were just so young when they got drafted to fight back then. Many of them got drafted right out of high school. Can you imagine going from playing high school football to holding a gun and killing another human being in a war?"

"I couldn't begin to understand," Bess answered.

"So you see, this letter was written many years ago," Evelyn continued, and she lowered the envelope with one hand while her other hand nervously stroked it like a feather. She looked at Bess and smiled. "I was in high school at the time. I was on the homecoming court and it was my senior year. The boy who took me to the homecoming dance was named Trent Dugan. He was a friend of a friend. He was so young and so handsome. His hair was thick and black and his eyes were dark and they just made me tingle when I stared at them. I barely knew him at the start of our date…but it turned out to be such a special night. He looked so handsome in his suit and of course I had my youthful beauty."

"Of course," Bess nodded with complete understanding of what Evelyn meant about fading beauty with age.

"So we danced together, in a way that was both awkward and romantic," Evelyn recalled. "We talked all the way through each song. We laughed and introduced each other to our friends. It was like…in that one night, we had found the other half to ourselves. We fit each other in every way and we knew it without even saying it. Sometimes love is like that you know. Sometimes it's a feeling and not just a lot of words."

"So what happened to this true love?" Bess asked.

"Oh we spent the summer together," Evelyn recalled. "We'd run around, go do things with our friends. We'd go swimming. We'd go bowling. We'd go roller skating. It was just a special summer for us to spend day after day with each other. Then one day, he got his letter from Uncle Sam. He had one month to pack, head down to North Carolina for basic training before he shipped off to war. I cried for a week. It was just a horrible way for the summer to end."

"I'm sure it was," Bess nodded, remembering more than one young man in her neighborhood who quite suddenly left when they were drafted.

"He was gone for three months when I got this in the mail. This letter was the only letter he wrote to me," Evelyn stated, waving the letter in the air. "A month later I saw in the newspaper that he died. I stayed in bed for days, holding this letter, and crying for my lost love."

"Well, then why would you leave something so precious in a book?" Bess asked. "I don't understand."

"Because I went on with my life," Evelyn said and she shifted in her chair like she was uncomfortable with this simple truth. "I found a good man. We settled down and had a family.

He was good to me and we had a wonderful life together. But I didn't love him as much as I loved Trent. I told myself it was because of my age. You know...our feelings are just so strong when we're young. When you're a teenager in love...it's very different than being an adult in love. Adult love is different in so many ways."

Bess could see Chet's face flash in her mind after hearing these words. She knew first hand how her love for Chet was different from the love she felt for her husband. Evelyn looked down at the envelope in her hands.

"For many years this letter has reminded me of my teenage love," Evelyn sighed. She ran her thumb over the envelope. "It's also been a reminder of a love I wasn't meant to have. My husband is dead now...and I feel like I should be remembering him more than I remember Trent. One day I was in the book room and I found this book of *Shakespeare's Sonnets* and I thought of Trent. I found the page in the book with one of Trent's favorite sonnets and I thought I'd put the envelope in there. It just seemed like a good place for his letter to go. No one ever reads Shakespeare in a retirement home, or so I thought. I felt it would be a fitting place to leave Trent's letter in the quiet confines of a book room. I even picked a high shelf so it wouldn't be found so easily. I never thought anyone would want to read this book, much less find it in here. I didn't realize you were such a fan of Shakespeare, Mrs. Bullock."

"I wasn't looking for a book by Shakespeare," Bess quickly explained. "The book was just there...lying on the floor. I simply picked up the book to return it to the shelf. That's when your letter fell out."

"The book was on the floor?" Evelyn asked, her voice indicating a hint of surprise in what Bess just told her. "That's impossible, Mrs. Bullock. I pushed that book far away from the edge of the shelf. It never should have fallen down."

"Well," Bess said, looking down at the book on her lap. "Somehow it worked its way off the shelf and onto the floor. That's where I found it."

"But how?" Evelyn asked, and she leaned forward in her seat.

Bess stood up and walked over to Evelyn. She handed her the book and the envelope.

"Perhaps it was the power of love," Bess suggested. "Maybe the power of love pushed that book right off the shelf. Maybe this letter wasn't meant to be left in a book, Evelyn. Maybe you were meant to keep it"

"I can't," Evelyn sighed, and she slowly caressed the envelope with her fingers. "I loved him so. If I close my eyes, I can see his young face smiling at me like I was the most beautiful part of his world. When I think of him…it just fills me with questions. You see, he was my one good chance to marry for love, Mrs. Bullock. When I see this letter…I think about that missed opportunity of my life. Did you ever lead your life asking yourself, "what if?" Mrs. Bullock?"

"On occasion," Bess nodded, the face of her baby Adam flashing in her mind. "I had my share of days to think about that question. Over time, I grew to be more focused on where my life is taking me rather than where my life has been."

"Whenever I see this letter…I think about the past," Evelyn said and she ended her comment by slowly shaking her head. "I can't keep this letter. I must focus on the memories of my husband, Mrs. Bullock. I'm not getting any younger and I want to make myself right with God before I die. I don't want to think about unrequited love. I want to think about the love of my marriage. I need to get rid of this letter...but in a way that is respectful to Trent's memory. Can you help me find a place for this letter? A place that will honor Trent's memory...but rid me of it for good."

Bess pondered the question. The nature of Evelyn's request caused Bess to grow silent.

It was an interesting problem to ponder.

"Well...burning it wouldn't be very respectful," Bess mumbled.

"He was a good soldier and a good man," Evelyn replied and she raised the letter in the air. "These words deserve a respectful end...not just a toss in the garbage. What can I do?"

Bess thought about the fact that she was asking for a respectful way to dispose of a letter from a soldier. It was a matter of military honor, Bess thought. The word "military" caused Bess to think of a possibility. In her mind she could see the face of one person she knew who had experience with honoring soldiers.

A PLACE WITH HONOR

The sun was not up when Bess heard her alarm clock ring. With the sound of bells filling her room, Bess managed to reach over and slam the palm of her hand directly on top of the alarm, shutting it off. She moved her hand off the clock and her fingers began to fumble across the nightstand for the switch to her light. When she found the switch, she flipped it on and quickly winced at the bright light that filled her room. She sat on the edge of the bed and yawned. When she was mildly awake she looked down at the end of her bed. There she found some clothes she had laid out the night before. Bess sat up and managed to slip on a sweater. She swung her legs off the bed and changed into a pair of slacks. She put on some socks and shoes and rubbed her eyes in one last attempt to wake up before she finally stood.

Bess let out another yawn when she reached the door and opened it. Outside the hallway was dim and empty. She quietly stepped out in the hallway and began her walk to Evelyn's room. While she walked, Bess couldn't remember the last time she was awake before the sun. A few nurses passed her in the hallways, but no residents were awake yet. All the doors to the rooms were still closed. A hush filled the hall. Bess turned a corner, yawned, and approached Evelyn's room. Unlike the other doors in the hallway, Bess noticed that Evelyn's door was wide open Bess looked inside to see Evelyn sitting in her chair with the envelope on her lap. Bess forced herself to smile despite her sleepy state. Evelyn didn't smile or say a word. Instead she stood up, walked out in the hallway and stopped in front of Bess.

"I'm ready," was all Evelyn said.

Together, both ladies walked down the dimly lit hallway. Bess was too tired to speak and, thankfully, Evelyn appeared to feel the same way. When they reached the door that led outside, Bess opened it and felt a chill of summer air nip her in the face. Bess had often started her days with a walk, but with the sun nipping at the horizon and not yet fully revealed, she knew this was going to be a brisk walk.

"A little cool out here," Evelyn mumbled while she rubbed her hands together.

"I agree," Bess replied, wishing she had brought her sweater along.

Their destination was an easy one to find. The flag pole Bess was looking for was quite prominent above the grounds of the Honey Hills Center. It was easily visible against the dark blue sky. She also noticed that there was no flag on the pole, which meant they were on time.

Together Bess and Evelyn followed a road that arced around the Honey Hills Center's main building. While they followed the road, Bess spied the barn in the distance and her thoughts drifted back to the young boy who ran away from the daycare room to look at the barn. The memory made her smile. Her thoughts quickly shifted when she spotted three older men standing around the flag pole. One of the men walked with a cane and held a flag that was folded like a triangle. The man carefully put his cane down and began to unfurl the American flag while two other men attached it to the pole. When the flag was hoisted up, Dutch Howard and the other men saluted the stars and stripes that hung from the pole.

"Who are they?" Evelyn asked as they approached the flag pole that was fixed next to a row of bushes.

"They," Bess announced with her first smile of the morning, "are the Flag Committee. They raise that flag every morning and take it down every evening. They are also war veterans and they've agreed to help us."

Together Bess and Evelyn quietly followed the road that led them to the flag pole. Bess was mindful of the thick dew on the grass and was hopeful that they wouldn't have to cross through the grass to get to the flag pole. Thankfully a cobblestoned path met the road, and Bess led Evelyn onto the pathway. At the end of the pathway was a small wooden bench. Bess and Evelyn stopped at the bench.

"Dutch!" Bess called out.

Dutch Howard waved at Bess and walked over to where she and Evelyn were standing. His face looked redder in the cool morning air, Bess thought. The sun struck his white hair and made it look almost luminous in the morning light. The silver eagle on his walking cane shone nearly as bright as his hair.

"Dutch…this is my friend I was telling you about. Her name is Evelyn," Bess said, pointing to Evelyn. "She brought the letter I told you about. The letter from that young soldier."

"May I see it," Dutch asked, sticking out his large hand.

Evelyn looked down at the envelope she was holding, and slowly handed it to Dutch. He grabbed it in a rather rough manner, checked the date on the envelope, and quickly opened the letter with the impatience of a child opening a present. He gripped the paper tightly while he read the letter, causing Evelyn's eyes to widen. Bess could only liken the look of concern on Evelyn's face to that of a child watching someone hold their favorite pet.

"Where did he fight?" Dutch grunted, still looking down at the letter.

"I believe it was in Southeast Asia," Evelyn managed to reply. "Lots of boys from my school were going over there to fight. Of course, I don't know where Trent was stationed over there. He wasn't there that long. That was his only letter to me. I'm afraid he died soon after writing it."

"I'm sorry," Dutch mumbled, and he folded the letter back up and stuffed it in the envelope. "Mrs. Bullock says you'd like to honor this young soldier's words and memory?"

"Yes, I would," Evelyn answered and she smiled a little after speaking.

Dutch pulled out a small clear plastic baggy from his pocket. He unzipped the baggie, slipped the envelope inside, and then zipped the baggie shut.

"I told Mrs. Bullock that we could do a small ceremony here," Dutch explained with his low gravely voice. "I brought a shovel. We could remove a piece of ground here, burry the letter next to the flag pole, and then replace the sod so no one would know. Is that alright with you, Evelyn?"

Bess watched Evelyn's eyes look around at the gardens that surrounded the flag pole.

She looked at the gazebo that sat just beyond the gardens. A small smile appeared on her face again and Bess thought the expression may have reflected a heart filled with relief and peace.

"Yes," Evelyn replied. "Yes, this would be a perfect place to honor Trent."

Dutch looked around to see if anyone else was out. Bess looked too but couldn't find anyone watching the Flag Committee at work. Dutch nodded to one of his men who grabbed hold of a shovel. The man placed the tip of the shovel onto the ground and pushed it down with his foot. The shovel easily sank into the soil. A layer of grass was carefully removed and placed to the side. Then another scoop of soil was pulled up from the hole and dumped onto a small pile right next to the hole. Dutch took the baggie that contained the envelope and placed it in the hole. Bess heard Evelyn let out a sigh.

"Are you okay, my dear?" Bess asked.

"Yes," Evelyn answered.

"Honor, duty, country," Dutch spoke and he lowered his head and folded his hands as if he were offering a prayer. "That was the motto for most of the young men and women who served in the armed forces when I served. We gather here this morning to honor one such young man. Because he perished on the battlefield, we honor his service this morning and we pray that this young man has found peace after serving his country when he was called. It is one thing to love a person…but quite another to love a country so much that you would lay down your life for it. That is what this young man has done and his country is forever grateful. Amen."

With those last words, the soil was dumped back into the hole and the layer of grass was neatly returned to its previous spot. Dutch laid his foot down on the sod and tramped on it to secure it to the soil.

"Thank you, Dutch," Bess said. "That was beautiful."

"Yes," Evelyn joined in. "Thank you so much."

"You're welcome, ladies" Dutch replied and he walked over and shook Evelyn's hand. "Would you two like to join us for some coffee? My wife, Nell, will be joining us, too."

"I think that sounds like a good idea," Bess said, suddenly mindful of the cool morning air that had wrapped itself around her. "How about you, Evelyn? Are you a coffee drinker?"

"No, thank you," Evelyn said and she slowly settled into a wooden bench close to where the flag pole was located. She sank down into the bench and stared down at the spot where Dutch so carefully covered the hole with dirt and sod. "I think I'd just like to sit, and think, and enjoy the beauty with Trent."

Bess smiled and nodded at Evelyn. It was one thing to say that she wanted to disconnect her heart from Trent, but they were just words. It was quite another to get a heart to let go of something it loved. Bess recalled the months after losing her infant son, Adam. When asked by friends and family, Bess always told them she was fine...but even to this day her heart still longed for her little boy. She understood the challenge of getting a heart to untether itself from feeling love for someone. Perhaps that was why she was comfortable leaving Evelyn alone.

"Thank you for your help, Mrs. Bullock," Evelyn said. "I think this was quite a good place for Trent to be."

"I think so too," Bess nodded.

Bess turned and followed Dutch and his friends back inside for some hot coffee. Her arms tingled from the cool air and she rubbed her hands quite vigorously. While the sun was beginning to make its presence known to the morning, it was clearly not warm enough for her. As she walked, Bess turned and looked up at the flag hanging loosely from the pole. For most residents, Bess thought, another day would begin when they saw that the American Flag had been successfully raised over the grounds of the Honey Hills Center. Yet, for a select few residents, what was just as important were the words of a young soldier secretly buried under that flag. Bess knew she would never look at that flag the same way without thinking of Trent's letter and his passionate words for the woman he loved.

THE SIGN IN THE GARDEN

The next day, after dinner, Chet and Bess went on an evening walk around the grounds of the Honey Hills Center. The heat from the sun was muted by a thin layer of wispy white clouds that wrapped across the sky like sheer lace. Bess slipped her hand into Chet's warm soft hand and smiled as they began their usual route. They made their way down the first street admiring the silence of the evening. There were the occasional chirps of birds, but the world sounded like it was now in quiet reflection at this point in the day. Bess glanced up at the flag pole and thought of Evelyn Short's words about love. She squeezed Chet's hand and her heart fluttered.

Moving down Meadow Avenue, Chet stopped and pointed out a squirrel in one yard who was trying to carry a rather large nut. Bess and Chet watched the squirrel dig quite furiously with his front paws before tucking the nut into the ground. They turned down Lark Lane where a rhododendron bush caused Bess to pause for a moment and admire the deep hues of violet that were prominently displayed on each limb.

A few more steps and they turned onto Dogwood Lane. They walked down the street where four ranch homes lined both sides of the street. Bess found her eyes drawn to one of the homes at the end of the street. A small red brick ranch home that sat at the corner of Dogwood Lane and Magnolia Avenue. It was the house that Bess always admired. The house that Chet knew she loved. Bess turned to Chet and they exchanged a smile. Suddenly, Bess wandered off the street and onto the front yard of one of the homes.

"Bess?" Chet said, following her into the yard. "Where are you going?"

"Follow me and you'll see," Bess said with a grin.

She led Chet in through the front yard of one house, then cut in between two other yards and around a home that had curtains drawn at the window. A woman sitting on her porch looked at Bess, who merely smiled and waved. A small rabbit darted out from under bush and Bess stumbled while she watched it charge off. She caught her balance and spotted her destination. Just ahead was the backyard to the vacant home on the corner. The house for sale with the two empty gardens in the backyard. Bess stepped into the yard and stopped next to the gardens, turned around and smiled at Chet who was trying to keep up.

"Bess!" Chet puffed, resting his hands on his narrow hips. He smiled but his face still held a look of confusion when he looked at her. "Why did you take off like that?"

"I followed my heart," Bess answered and she laughed a little after her words. "I know it sounds silly, Chet. Of course it would have been more sensible to stay on our route and continue to walk…but sometimes a heart isn't sensible. Sometimes a heart will act in ways that don't make sense to anyone. My heart wanted me to cut through the grass and stop right here so I could show you something."

"What?" Chet asked, stepping closer to the garden.

Bess pointed to a small sign she had made and planted in the middle of one of the gardens. It was a small note card that she attached to a wooden ruler. She had stuck the sign in the ground earlier in the morning. She wrote the words "Bess Bullock's Garden" on the sign with a red marker. She watched

Chet smile when he read the words. The look of confusion on his face slowly faded like the wispy clouds in the sky.

"I once told you that an unused garden is like an unused life. How when I look at an empty garden all I can think about are the lost possibilities of that garden." Bess said and she nudged some of the dirt in the garden with the tip of her shoe. "I don't want my heart to be an empty garden, Chet. I don't want to sit around and just think about the possibilities of what might grow there if I married you. My heart is telling me to say yes to these gardens. It's telling me to say yes to this house. It's telling me to say yes to the man with the kindest eyes and the softest hands I'll ever know. Yes, Chet….my heart is telling me to say yes to you and your proposal to marry me."

Chet grinned. He stepped over to Bess and gave her a soft kiss. They wrapped their arms around each other and stood next to the two empty gardens. The veil of clouds lifted. Golden sunlight filled their eyes. Bess could feel her heart race and her toes tingle. She had left the comfort of a path laid before her by life. She had trusted her heart and wandered onto a new path laid out by love. Somewhere along this new path she hoped to find the good things that would come from love.

THE APPOINTMENT

It took a few days for Bess to get used to the idea of being known as Mrs. Wooden. She marveled at the fact that no matter what her age, she still got butterflies in her stomach when she thought about the idea of marriage. The first thing that changed once she accepted his proposal was that Chet wanted to walk with her twice a day and not just once. Bess was happy with that change and found they still had a lot to talk about. Increasing the number of walks also meant that they passed the home Bess longed for twice a day. Soon, they both realized it was something they could no longer ignore. One morning, while walking by the home, Chet announced he would make a few phone calls to inquire about the home. His inquiry soon turned into a date on which he and Bess would meet with someone about purchasing the home.

Early one morning, Bess and Chet met in front of the office of Mr. Howard Jenkins. Mr. Jenkins was the Human Resource Manager for the Honey Hills Center. He was also in charge of dealing with couples that wished to move into the Honey Hills Center's independent living homes. Chet explained that interviewing couples who wished to purchase one of the independent living homes was part of Mr. Jenkins's job.

Bess and Chet stood in the hallway for a moment. Bess stared at the dark wood grain of the door and then she felt Chet's fingers lace around her hand.

"Are you okay, Twinkle Toes?" Chet asked. It was a nickname he gave Bess after the first time she attended a meeting of the Waltzing Club. It was also a nickname that always made Bess smile.

"I'm nervous," Bess laughed.

"All we can do is ask," Chet replied with a soft calming voice. "If they say no...we'll just continue to live the way we have been."

"I know," Bess nodded. "It's just that...behind that door...our future is behind that door, Chet. It makes me nervous to think about walking through it."

"It makes me excited," Chet replied and he quickly grabbed the door knob and opened it.

Once inside they found an office with two large windows filled with sunlight. Green potted plants lined the ledge to the windows. Hunter green carpet spread out along the floor. A bookshelf fit snuggly in one corner of the room. In another corner, Bess spotted a couch and table that she thought looked quite inviting for someone to sit and enjoy coffee or tea. On the other side of the room was a large oak desk where a young man was sitting. He quickly stood up, revealing his navy blue dress pants, shiny black shoes, and a white dress shirt. He scratched his thick black hair and adjusted the red tie that swung across his bright white shirt.

"Mr. Wooden," the young man said shaking Chet's hand. "Nice to see you again."

The young man turned to Bess and extended his hand.

"My name is Howard Jenkins," he announced. "You must be Mrs. Bullock. I've heard a lot about you from Mr. Wooden. Please sit down."

Bess and Chet settled into a pair of large maroon leather chairs that were fixed across from Mr. Jenkins' desk. She watched Mr. Jenkins slip on some glasses and grab some papers. Bess thought it was a little funny that she and Chet, who were clearly much older than Mr. Jenkins, now needed permission from this young man to follow their hearts. She was also a bit concerned at how serious Mr. Jenkins appeared. How he didn't crack a smile when they walked in and still didn't smile at them while he prepared his papers. She was already nervous about the meeting and his demeanor was making her even more nervous. She thought of a way to put Mr. Jenkins at ease and to create a more relaxed atmosphere.

Bess quickly glanced on the shelf behind his desk and spotted some picture frames filled with faces of a smiling young boy and a smiling young girl. They both had blond hair and appeared to be about four or five years of age. She guessed they were his children. She also spotted one picture of a blond haired woman smiling with the two children and she also guessed this was his family.

"You have a lovely family," Bess said with a smile.

The comment caused Mr. Jenkins to turn in his seat and look over his shoulder at the pictures. When he turned back to Bess his rigid face had melted into a smile.

"Thank you," Mr. Jenkins grinned. "They keep me busy."

"Young children will do that," Bess nodded. "I would guess my granddaughter is about the same age as your daughter and I wish I had her energy."

"I agree, Mrs. Bullock," Mr. Jenkins. "When I get home and they run to the door...I think the same thing about my children. I wish I had that much energy."

Bess nodded at his observation, happy to see he was no longer so serious, but a smiling young father and husband. She was also happy that they found common ground on something. Perhaps, she thought, this would bode well for what was to come.

"So you have an eye on one of our homes," Mr. Jenkins said, the smile quickly fading.

"We do," Chet replied, glancing over at Bess. "The one on Dogwood Lane. I believe it's been vacant for quite some time."

"That it has," Mr. Jenkins said and then he grew silent while he read a paper. He put the paper to the side, sat up in his chair and looked across the desk at Chet and Bess and smiled.

"It does cost money to purchase one of our homes," Mr. Jenkins advised.

"How much for the house on Dogwood Lane?" Chet asked.

Bess watched Mr. Jenkins write something down on a piece of paper and slide it across the desk to Chet. Bess watched Chet pick up the paper, look at the number, nod, and then slide the paper back.

"That shouldn't be a problem," Chet mumbled. "My attorney is Dale Babbot. I'll call him today and have the money sent over. When would be able to move in?"

"Once I speak with Mr. Babbot...you should be able to move in by the end of the week," Mr. Jenkins replied.

Bess managed to catch a glimpse at the number on the paper and the number of zeros she saw made her start to cough. She didn't even have half of that amount in her bank account. She looked at Chet and she could feel her mind begin to race. There were still things about Chet that she didn't know, and this instance was a reminder of that. Even though she loved him, it made her a little nervous to think that she didn't know everything about him.

"Then I think we may proceed," Mr. Jenkins replied. He pulled out some papers and pens. "I'll need both of you to sign and date these papers. This is an agreement of payment in full for the house. Now before you sign...a word of advice. In signing these papers you two are making a joint commitment to this home...and each other. We've never really had unmarried couples move into one of our independent living homes before. Now as you both are well aware, we do embrace the Christian faith here at Honey Hills. We have church worship at our chapel. We welcome church leaders who come to visit from time to time. With all that in mind, I must ask a rather personal question of both of you. Is there intent to marry?"

"Yes," Chet and Bess both answered at the same time.

Bess turned and looked at Chet. Chet was already looking at her. They both laughed at the timing of their answer.

"Very well," Mr. Jenkins said and he tapped his hand on some papers on his desk. "I've read reports from the nurses in both of your hallways and they have no evidence to show that either of you are suffering from any type of dementia."

"You did background checks on us?" Bess laughed, recalling her days as a police officer.

"It's standard procedure," Mr. Jenkins replied. "We have to make sure our residents are of sound mind when making such a big decision. The reports on you two back that up. In fact, the nurses say you both have very sharp minds, which is what we want in making this kind of decision. With these testimonies, and after speaking with both of you...I do hereby grant this request given that both of you are of sound minds and judgment."

"I would like to think this is being granted more because of sound hearts than sound minds," Bess added. "After all, marriage is more about the heart than the mind, don't you agree Mr. Jenkins."

"Yes I do, Mrs. Bullock," Mr. Jenkins smiled for the first time in their meeting. "Once you sign these papers...I think that will take care of our business."

"How soon before the house is ready?" Chet asked.

"About a week," Mr. Jenkins answered. "I'd like to give maintenance time to clean, repair a few things, and make it as good as new for you two."

"So we have one week to pack?" Bess asked, trying not to sound all that panicked.

"As soon as you sign the papers," Mr. Jenkins stated.

Bess and Chet both scooped up their pens and signed where Mr. Jenkins had asked them. Bess squeezed the pen tightly, almost afraid it would slip from her fingers. She carefully put the pen tip to paper and wrote her name. With one swift stroke of the pen, Bess could feel her heart race and a broad smile began to spread across her cheeks. She put the pen down and took a deep breath. It occurred to her that something quite surprising had just happened in the seconds it took her and Chet to write their names. In the heart of the Honey Hills Center, in a place that prided itself on making each day the same for its residents, a change had occurred with the stroke of a pen. A change that Bess knew was for the better.

"Change is good," Bess whispered to herself.

THE POSSIBILITIES OF DOGWOOD LANE

The following week Bess received a phone call from Mr. Jenkins congratulating her on the purchase of the home on Dogwood Lane. He stated that he cleared things with Chet's attorney and that the house was ready for them to move in. Later in the morning, Bess pulled out her suitcases and began to pack her things. It didn't seem all that long ago when Bess first moved into the Honey Hills Center and unpacked her suitcases for what she thought was the final time. As was often the case, life surprised her with other plans.

Like the day she moved in, Bess made a phone call to ask her family for help with packing. Her daughter, Samantha, and her granddaughter, Nicole, were there in an instant. Together the three ladies quietly went about folding Bess's clothes and putting them in boxes. While Nicole had a lot to say, Samantha was surprisingly quiet while she worked. Knowing her daughter, Bess could tell she was upset about what was happening.

"Grandma," Nicole said. She ran over to Bess, her head bumping against Bess's hip. Nicole held up a silk scarf with butterflies on it and twirled the scarf in the air. "Can I have this one, grandma?"

"Nicole!" Samantha snapped with an angry tone.

"It's okay," Bess said with a wave of her hand. She gently wrapped the scarf around Nicole's neck two times and then tapped her once on the nose with her finger. "Don't you look like a princess? Of course you can have it."

"Thank you, Granny," Nicole giggled and she gave Bess a hug before diving into another set of drawers. "I can spell scarf, Granny? Wanna hear? S-C-A-R-F."

Bess smiled and clapped for Nicole. Bess forgot how the early years in elementary school led young children to spell everything to impress grown-ups. Whenever Nicole would spell a word Bess always cheered her on and gave her hugs, just as she had done for Samantha many years earlier. However, Bess knew it would take more than a scarf to make her daughter happy. While she wasn't objecting to the move, Bess could tell Samantha wasn't pleased with the decision.

"Are you sure about this move, Mother?" Samantha asked while she folded some slacks and placed them on a pile. "I mean…Mr. Wooden seems like a nice man from the times I've met him. Moving in together…well that's a big step."

"He's a good man," Bess replied while she lowered a pile of sweaters in a suitcase.

"But why, Mom?" Samantha asked and she carried a packed box over to Bess's bed. "Why do you have to live in a home again? We just sold your other house. I think it will be too much work for you to maintain a house for you and Mr. Wooden. I mean…you're both in your eighties."

"The Honey Hills' staff is very helpful," Bess quickly explained. "They cut the grass. If we have problems with a light or a stove, we call the Honey Hills Center and someone comes to fix it. They'll even sweep and dust for us once a week."

"I don't know, Mother," Samantha sighed and she tapped her long finger nails on the side of a suitcase. "I just don't like it. I just don't think it's safe. What would Dad say?"

"Your father never wanted me to be alone," Bess replied and she sat down on the bed and took

Samantha's hand and kissed the top of it. "At this point in my life…love is different than it was when I was a young woman. You see, when you're young…love is about attraction and intimacy and passion and all those other things that can cloud your mind and your judgment. When you get to be my age, love is less complicated. It's no longer about passion and more about finding someone who will share every day with you. For me, love isn't about physical intimacies anymore. Love is about finding someone you want to talk to, or hold hands with, or laugh with or share a day with. That is the kind of love I have been sharing with Chet. Now with this move we can have a bit more privacy to continue to share our days and our love."

"Aren't you happy being alone?" Samantha asked. "You can come and go as you please. You don't need to check in with anyone. Since my divorce I've really grown to enjoy not having anyone to keep tabs on me. I thought you'd feel the same way since you moved here."

"I did," Bess answered. "You know I was sixty when your father died. I've been alone for two decades, Samantha. Yes, I had my years of independence to enjoy. However, my heart has changed after being alone for so long. A dear man named Chet Wooden has changed my heart. I'd like to embrace that change and see where it takes me. Right now…it's taking me to Dogwood Lane."

"Are you going to…marry him?" Samantha asked.

"That's usually what people do when they get engaged," Bess replied. She looked at Samantha and smiled. "It won't be for a couple months. We have family out in California. It may take your uncle a little time to make the trip east for a wedding."

"I…" Samantha started to say and her voice trailed off.

"He's a good man," Bess said and she took Samantha's hands in her own. "He makes me happy and I love him. At this point in my life, that's all any woman could ask for."

"Mom, I just worry about you," Samantha said and she wrapped her arm around Bess's shoulders and hugged her for the first time in a long while.

"You worry too much, Samantha," Bess sighed. "You always have. When you were a little girl I remember how you'd worry about Santa, and the Easter Bunny, and Leprechauns at the end of a rainbow. You worried about things that most children never thought that much about. That's who you are, Samantha. That's what makes you such a great mother, too. We both know worrying is what separates a great mother from a good one...right, dear?"

Samantha looked at her mother and smiled. From that smile Bess realized there would be no fighting with Samantha over this decision. It was like seeing a white flag in the form of a happy face. Even though she was divorced, Samantha could still understand love and the ways of one's heart. It appeared that she wasn't going to try to change the direction of Bess's heart in this matter. It also made Bess happy to know that Samantha could still believe in the possibilities of love.

Later in the evening, Bess prepared to spend her last night in her room. With her pajamas on, she settled in front of her TV and watched the news when she heard a knock on the door. Bess grabbed her robe and slipped it on then headed for the door. When she opened the door, she was surprised to find Chef Tony standing in the hallway. He was holding a bag in one hand and some cook books in the other.

"I'm sorry, Mrs. Bullock," Tony said. "I just wanted you to be the first to know that I'm gonna be leaving at the end of tomorrow."

"Leaving?" Bess asked while a freshly baked croissant flashed in her head. She closed her eyes, shook her head and smiled at Tony. "Well, given how many chefs we've had at the Honey Hills...I can't say the news comes as much of a surprise. Where will you go, Tony?"

"There's a resort in the Catskills of New York. They want me to come and work for them," Tony announced. "It was all very sudden. I guess their head chef quit and they contacted my college for a name to recommend. I called the resort last night and was told that I'll be their head chef. I'll also have a staff of ten working under me in their kitchen. They told me they attract lots of tourists during the summer and that they also have lots of skiers who stay at the resort during the winter. They even hold corporate retreats for top executives."

"It sounds like an important job to me," Bess nodded and she smiled at how quickly he spoke and the urgency in his voice. "I'd imagine your grandmother would have been very proud of you, Tony."

"Grandma Cordaro always wanted us grandchildren to do work that helped others," Chef Tony recalled. "I did that here...and it felt good. I'll always have good memories of this place."

"So why leave? Why does a young man like you need this kind of job?" Bess asked.

"College loans," Chef Tony quickly answered. "I have bills to pay, Mrs. Bullock. This new job gives me a better chance at taking care of those loans."

"Well, then, you're quite lucky," Bess nodded. "We've all enjoyed your cooking here at Honey Hills. I'm afraid you've spoiled us with all of the things you've made. Do you know who your replacement will be?"

"I put in a good word for Willie," Tony said. "He knows all my recipes. He's quick to learn what I taught him about cooking. I think they're going to give him a chance before considering other applicants."

The news made Bess smile. As she listened to Chef Tony talk excitedly about his salary, the four-star resort he was about to be employed by, and his eagerness to explore the Catskills, Bess couldn't help but smile. The way he spoke, the excitement in his voice, the passion he shared about the changes in his life just made Bess feel giddy inside. While she wasn't moving to the Catskills, Bess began to feel the same kind of excitement about the change in her life. What possibilities awaited her at Dogwood Lane?

TWO WEEKS LATER

She rose early, before the sun. She rose in darkness, careful not to wake Chet. She quietly slipped out of bed, dressed and smiled while she thought about her morning.

A minute later, Bess sat in her kitchen, made herself a bowl of oatmeal and topped it off with milk and banana. As she sat at her kitchen table, she found that her eyes tended to linger out the kitchen window. She could see a dark blue sky growing lighter at the horizon, and with that light, her view of the backyard started to fill with greater colors and details. While she chewed her food and sipped her juice, Bess could feel her heart race. It was the first day of summer. It was also her first morning to work in her gardens and she was excited to start.

After breakfast, she stepped out to her garage. She grabbed a small hand shovel, gardening gloves, and a pad to kneel on while working over her garden. Carrying her tools for work, she opened the door leading from her garage to her backyard and stopped in the doorway.

She looked up and let the first summer sun of the season strike her face. Even though it was quite early in the morning, Bess was amazed at how warm the rays of light were that fell on her face. Her eyes turned down to the green grass that lay just beyond her feet. She let her gaze drift along the dark green yard, following its slope up to where two gardens awaited her attention. From where she stood, the gardens resembled brown mounds of dirt with a few tangles of dried grass and weeds that had survived the winter. In the far corner of the yard, a tree provided some shade from the warm sunshine. Bess drew in a deep breath and smiled.

"Here we go," she giggled to herself.

Bess took her first step and watched her foot sink into the blades of grass. With one foot into her new backyard, Bess felt like a school girl dipping her toe into a pool. She smiled and then began to stride into her yard for the first time. When she reached her gardens, Bess stood and surveyed the two brown rectangles on either side of her. She looked left, then right, then left again. Both gardens were in dire need of removing dead growth from the previous owner.

"Time to work," Bess told herself. She turned to one of the gardens, dropped her bag of gardening tools, and slipped on her gloves. She reached down and grabbed hold of a brown weed. She gave it a tug and the weed snapped out of the ground root and all. She carefully placed it in the grass next to her before pulling out a few more weeds. As the pile grew, so did the smile on her face. The smell of the dirt. The crackling sound of dry grass and weeds. The slow process of restoring life to a small patch of dirt had now begun.

The beauty of gardening, Bess thought, was that each season was unique. Each year something different could be planted. Different colors would blossom. New life would replace the life that had bloomed in the previous season.

The thought reminded Bess of something she had read in a gardening magazine. An article she found that stated how a garden is a true reflection of the heart of the gardener. How the things that were planted, the shades and the colors, could provide some insight into the soul of a gardener.

As she dug and cleared out the old things from her garden, Bess began to realize how true this motto was. She stood and looked at both of her gardens for a moment. She knew it didn't matter what she planted in them. She knew her gardens would reflect her heart in one important way. In her gardens, life would return. Beauty would flourish. Colors would fade. Life would end. New life would return again. There would be changes in the gardens that Bess would keep. Changes in her gardens that, like the changes in her life, made Bess excited about her future. It also made her anxious to begin planting for a new season. As she pondered what to plant in her new gardens, one question slipped from her lips.

"What flowers would look nice for a wedding?"

FRIENDS

One July morning Bess was knee deep in her garden when she realized it was Tuesday. She had completely forgotten about Bridge Club. At that moment, Chet called out to remind her of the time. Bess came into her house, washed up, kissed Chet goodbye and quickly walked two blocks to the Honey Hills Center.

Stepping into the building was like slipping on something warm and comfortable. Her eyes dropped down to the familiar sky blue rug. She began to walk through the halls, glancing up at the same paintings that hung on the walls when she lived there. She heard the low hum of the air conditioning system that kept the center cool on warm summer days. She even smiled at a few nurses before turning at a corner that led to the book room.

Bess could feel her smile fade when her eyes came upon a surprising sight. She found her friends gathered outside the book room and not inside as she expected. Through one of the windows, Bess could see a small group was seated around the table where Bess and her friends usually met to play cards.

"Good morning," Bess said, stepping over to her friends. "What's going on in there?"

"Puzzle club," Flo grumbled. "They got here before us and they say that they're starting on a new puzzle. They won't be done for hours."

"Puzzle club?" Bess asked. She turned her head and looked in through the doorway. She spied a familiar looking walking cane with a bright silver eagle perched on the top of the cane. "Is Dutch Howard in there?"

"Yes," Rose said and her eyes turned towards the table.

Bess stepped into the room and spotted Dutch seated in the middle of the group. Silence filled the room as the Puzzle Club members were focused on assembling the small pieces scattered across the table. Bess thought of a way to get Dutch's attention and then loudly cleared her throat. Dutch looked over and Bess quickly waved him out of the room. His bright red face didn't even crack a smile at the sight of Bess. His eyes narrowed and he appeared clearly annoyed that she was calling him away from the rest of the group.

"Dutch," Bess began. "What are you doing here?"

"Our puzzle club is meeting, Mrs. Bullock," Dutch replied.

"But our Bridge Club has usually met here on a Tuesday morning," Bess explained. "I believe your puzzle club always met on another day."

"Wednesdays," Dutch nodded. "You're right, Mrs. Bullock, we used to meet on Wednesdays. Then we had a new member join our club and they told us that Tuesday morning would be a better day for them to meet. It wasn't a problem for anyone else in our group, so we decided to change the meeting to Tuesday mornings."

"Who is the new member you're talking about?" Bess asked.

"I think you know her," Dutch began.

"Dutch!" a woman's voice called out with a familiar tone of helplessness that Bess quickly recognized. Bess looked in the room and saw the face of Lillian Peck looking towards the doorway and holding a small puzzle piece high in the air.

"Dutch! I need your help, Dutch! I can't find where this piece goes" she continued to call out.

"She's not too good at putting puzzles together," Dutch sighed. "But as the president of the Puzzle Club...I'm teaching her everything I know."

Dutch took a deep breath, turned, and stepped back into the room with his walking cane. Bess smiled when she saw Dutch walk over to Lillian and assist her with the puzzle. Indeed, Bess thought, Lillian had moved on to another man. Perhaps, Bess observed, this was a sign that Lillian had moved on from Chet. Perhaps she had set her sights on Dutch instead.

"Maybe we should just cancel Bridge Club for this week," Rose suggested.

"Is the game room open?" Alma asked.

"I'm afraid not," Rose replied.

"Well...I for one would like to play Bridge this morning," Flo mumbled.

"What do you think, Bess?" Rose asked. "Do you want to play?"

"Change," Bess said to herself.

"What did you say, Bess?" Rose asked.

Bess slowly looked around at her friends and gave each one of them a smile.

"Come with me," Bess said, stepping away from the book room. She looked around at the faces of her friends. "You heard me, ladies...come with me."

Flo, Rose, and Alma looked at each other. One by one they followed Bess, trusting in what their friend was asking them to do. Rose, the oldest of the ladies, was the first to follow Bess. Alma, the newest member of their bridge club was next. Flo was the last and most reluctant one to follow.

"Where are we going, Bess?" Flo asked, standing up. "Do you know some place where we can go and play cards?"

"I thought that instead of playing cards this morning…we could go for a walk," Bess announced and she finished off her idea with a wide smile. She turned to see that her smile was not returned from the curious faces following behind her.

"It's a lovely morning," Bess urged. "I think it would be nice for us to walk together."

Striding down the hallway, Bess tried to ignore the silence that her idea was greeted with. She found the nearest exit and quickly led her group of reluctant walkers outside. Sunlight splashed in her face and caused Bess to squint when she opened the door. The air was crisp and dry and the warmth of the sun seemed to make the morning quite comfortable.

"Where are we going?" Rose asked from behind.

"I said we are going for a walk," Bess called out.

"I know that," Rose nodded. "I just wanted to know…where are we walking to?"

"Nowhere special," Bess replied. She turned, looked at her friends and smiled again.

"Don't you think it's a wonderful morning, ladies? I think it looks rather pretty. My father always said that a good walk in the morning was like shaking hands with a new day. Besides, why shouldn't a group of friends go for a walk together?"

"Because it's Tuesday," Flo grumbled, trying to keep up with the group. "It's the morning we play cards, Bess. Now let's go back inside."

"Cards have brought us together," Bess said and she stopped and turned to her friends. "It is our bond as friends…but as friends…we can still do other things together."

"I would have brought my sweater if I knew we were going to take a walk," Rose grumbled and she rubbed her hands together to emphasize her point.

"Me too," Flo chimed in with her arms wrapped around her chest.

"We'll make it a short walk so no one gets cold," Bess promised and she turned and began to lead them down the road.

"I, for one, think it's a splendid morning for a walk," Alma Crisp finally spoke up. "We spend too many days inside. A little fresh air never hurt anyone."

"I don't mind walking," Rose stated. She quickly moved to the front of the group and stopped in front of Bess, causing her to stop, too. "Bess we're on an empty street in the middle of the Honey Hills grounds. If I knew we were doing this, I would have worn more comfortable shoes. Where did you say we are going again?"

"Maybe we will walk in one big circle," Bess suggested. "Perhaps we will come right back to where we begin. For me, a good walk is not so much about where it begins or where it ends. It is about what happens along the way, ladies. Hearing birds chirp in the trees. Seeing colorful flowers that line a garden. Passing familiar faces that smile at you and allow you to smile back. These are the things that make a good walk for me…and I wanted to share these good things with you….because you're my friends."

Her words stopped all three ladies in their tracks. Bess turned and looked back at them. Alma smiled and seemed to wipe her eyes with the back of her hand. Rose smiled and nodded her approval to Bess. Even Flo found her lips were curving into a smile. Each woman reached out and grabbed hold of the other's hand. Bess felt Alma's hand slip between her fingers.

"Show us, Bess," Alma said. "Show us where you walk…and share the beautiful things you see every morning."

Bess turned and began to lead her friends down the street. She pointed to a tree at the corner of Dogwood and Magnolia Streets, where a bright red cardinal chirped quite cheerfully every morning. One block later, they moved by some rose bushes that were so sweet they filled her nose like candy. Along both sides of the street, Bess commented on the crisp green grass that had returned with the season. When they walked under a large oak tree, the wind picked up.

Bess stopped her friends, pointed up to the tree and closed her eyes as the sound of rustling leaves filled the moment. When she opened her eyes, she saw how her friends had also closed their eyes to listen to the same sounds that rode on the passing breeze. When they opened their eyes, their faces looked as pleased as Bess felt.

"I think this will be a good walk," Bess announced.

All three ladies didn't speak, but they smiled and continued to follow Bess. Together, Bess thought, they shook the morning's hand. More importantly, they made it a good walk not because of what they saw, or what they heard, but because they took this walk together.

THE END

ABOUT THE AUTHOR

Allen B. Boyer is the author of two Young Adult novels and one nonfiction book about the West Point Academy and its famous graduates. His books have been sold around the country. This is his second cozy mystery novel. The first—*Gumshoe Granny Investigates*—introduced Bess Bullock, the protagonist of the Retirement Home Mystery series.

Mr. Boyer lives near Hershey, Pennsylvania, with his wife, Suzanne, and their three children. He likes to take his children and their dog to visit residents at a nearby retirement home.